For Bess –  J.D.

For Phil –  J.S.

First published in 2003 by Macmillan Children's Books
a division of Macmillan Publishers Limited
20 New Wharf Road, London N1 9RR
Basingstoke and Oxford
Associated companies worldwide
www.panmacmillan.com

ISBN 0 333 96442 X (HB)
ISBN 0 333 96443 8 (PB)

Text copyright © 2003 Julia Donaldson
Illustrations copyright © 2003 Joel Stewart
Moral rights asserted

3 5 7 9 8 6 4 2

A CIP catalogue record for this book is available
from the British Library.

Printed in Belgium by Proost

The Magic Paintbrush

Written by **Julia Donaldson**   Illustrated by **Joel Stewart**

MACMILLAN
CHILDREN'S BOOKS

Go and catch some shrimps, Shen.
Go and catch some fish.
Go and gather oysters
To fill the empty dish."

Shen sits on the seashore.
A stick is in her hand.
She sits there drawing pictures,
Pictures in the sand.

She draws a flower, a flying fish,
She draws a boat at sea,
A hen, a hare, a dancing dog,
A weeping willow tree.

The waves roll in and wash away
The pictures in the sand.
But on a rock there sits a man.
A brush is in his hand.

He looks around. He calls to Shen.
"Come here!" he whispers. "Hush!
We don't want all the world to know
About this magic brush."

He slips the brush into her hand
And tells her to be sure
Never to paint for wealthy folk
But only for the poor.

"Did you catch some shrimps, Shen?
Did you catch some fish?
Did you gather oysters
To fill the empty dish?"

"No shrimps, no fish, no oysters!"
Shen laughs and runs inside.
She paints a pot, then stands and waits
Until the paint has dried.

The paint dries on the paper.
The painting of the pot
Is not a painting any more,
But real, and steaming hot.

"The pot is full of shrimps, Shen!
The pot is full of fish!
The pot is full of oysters
To fill the empty dish!"

The village people hear the news.
Into the house they crush.
The young and old all want to see
Shen and her magic brush.

She paints a melon for a boy,
A ladder for a man,
A basket for a woman,
And for a girl, a fan.

And soon the news spreads far and wide
And people stand in queues
For blankets, boats and buffaloes,
For hats and coats and shoes.

The news spreads over fields of rice
And over desert sands,
Until at last, inside Shen's house
The powerful Emperor stands.

"I order you to paint a tree
And make it very big.
Instead of leaves, paint golden coins,
A hundred on each twig."

Shen shakes her head. "Your Majesty,
I promised to be sure
Never to paint for wealthy folk
But only for the poor."

The Emperor scowls and stamps his foot.
He bellows to his men,
"Seize the magic paintbrush
And seize the girl called Shen."

Now Shen sits in a prison
Upon a cold stone floor.
She waits there till the Emperor
Opens the prison door.

He holds the magic paintbrush.
He orders, "Paint that tree!
Paint me my tree of golden coins
And then you shall go free."

Shen takes the brush, and bowing low
Says, "Gracious Majesty,
Come back here in the morning
And you shall have your tree."

That night the Emperor lies in bed
And dreams about his tree,
While Shen is busy painting
A horse and then a key.

The key turns in the prison door
And Shen stands free outside.
She climbs on to the horse's back
And swiftly starts to ride.

"Where are my coins?" the Emperor shouts.
"Where is my golden tree?
 Where is the magic brush?" he cries.
"Who let the girl go free?"

He climbs on to his fastest horse
And rides with all his men.
Over the fields and desert sands
They gallop after Shen.

"It's Shen! It's Shen! She's back again!"
The neighbours gather round.
But Shen is painting silently
While distant hoofbeats sound.

She paints a mighty river.
A river deep and wide.
The Emperor and all his men
Stop on the other side.

The Emperor scowls and stamps his foot.
He shakes his fist at Shen.
"I'll swim across your river,
And so will all my men."

But Shen is busy painting.
A beast with scales and claws.
Its scarlet wings are open
And flames curl from its jaws.

"My dragon needs a tail," says Shen,
"And then it will be real.
Yes, then it will be roaring
And ready for a meal.

"Now shall I paint that tail?" she asks.
"Or would you rather go?"
She dips her brush into the pot.
The Emperor cries out, "No!"

He turns his horse and rides away.
Away ride all his men.
Shen takes the magic paintbrush
And starts to paint again.

She paints a mound of golden rice
And cakes like little moons,
And drums and flutes, till all the streets
Ring out with merry tunes.

The sun goes down. The moon comes out
And shines as bright as day
While Shen and all the villagers
Dance the night away.

Contents

NB: because Switzerland's resorts vary in their interest according to the season, we have given star ratings for winter and for summer

This book employs a simple rating system to help choose which places to visit:

✓	'top ten'

◆◆◆	do not miss
◆◆	see if you can
◆	worth seeing if you have time

INTRODUCTION

Whoever coined the phrase 'the best things in life are free' cannot have had Switzerland in mind. The visitor to this tiny country, located in the heart of Europe, will certainly find all that's best… the most breathtaking mountain scenery it is possible to imagine; some of the world's most luxurious and stylish hotels; winter sports resorts that are without equal; a transportation system that is the envy of the world; and picturesque villages and towns. But far from being 'free', Switzerland's myriad attractions are almost without exception on the expensive side.

However, when you consider the quality of food, service and accommodation, the excellent safety record of skilifts and cable cars, the efficiency in ensuring safety on the piste, the high reputation of Swiss ski schools, the charm of the mountain villages, and the sophistication and beauty of the lakeside cities and towns, there can be little doubt that a trip to Switzerland really is worth the extra cost.

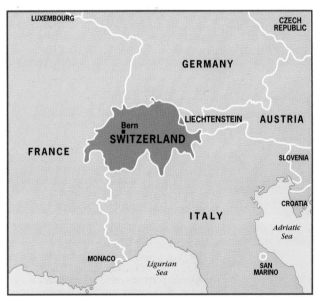

Essential
Switzerland

by
GERRY CRAWSHAW

Gerry Crawshaw is an experienced travel
writer. He writes for numerous magazines and
journals, and has also written guides to a
variety of countries.

AA

Produced by AA Publishing

Written by Gerry Crawshaw
Peace and Quiet section
by Paul Sterry

Revised second edition © July
1995
First published 1991

Edited, designed and produced
by AA Publishing. © The
Automobile Association 1995.
Maps © The Automobile
Association 1995.

Distributed in the United Kingdom
by AA Publishing, Norfolk House,
Priestley Road, Basingstoke,
Hampshire, RG24 9NY.

ISBN 0 7495 1109 5

Published by AA Publishing, a
trading name of Automobile
Association Developments
Limited, whose registered office is
Norfolk House, Priestley Road,
Basingstoke, Hampshire,
RG24 9NY.
Registered number 1878835.

Colour separation: L C Repro,
Aldermaston.

Printed by: Printers Trento, S.R.L.,
Italy

Front cover picture: Grindelwald

Country Distinguishing Signs

On maps, international
distinguishing signs indicate the
location of countries around
Switzerland. Thus:

(AUS) = Austria
(F) = France
(D) = Germany
(I) = Italy
(FL) = Liechtenstein

BACKGROUND

Landlocked in the middle of Europe and conditioned by its historic evolution, Switzerland has four national languages. The German-speaking area north of the Alps is by far the largest, and here Swiss-German is a spoken dialect with the added flavour of local variants. In the French-speaking regions of the southwest there is a marked French touch, while south of the Alps the waving palms of the Ticino herald the Italian tongue and way of life. In the pockets of southeast Switzerland, the Grisons (also known as the Graubunden), an ancient Latin tongue, Rhaeto-Romanic (Romansch), has survived right through the centuries.

It was from the Helvetians, a Celtic tribe which inhabited these parts in pre-Christian times, that Switzerland inherited the name Helvetia, which still appears on Swiss stamps. The official name 'Confederatio Helvetica' is embossed on all coins and, abbreviated to CH, is carried on all motor vehicles. Although the Helvetians became integrated into the Roman Empire, they nevertheless retained their tribal autonomy. Along the centuries, through the fiefdoms of the feudal system into a growing union of small states to form one confederation, none of the units lost its autonomy; and it is this structural fragmentation of living cells that characterises Switzerland to this day.

Mountains have conditioned the Swiss character and Swiss history. The Romans built the trans-Alpine routes which became the reasons – to have and to keep – for Switzerland's existence. Not unnaturally, therefore, Switzerland was born at the foot of the St Gotthard massif when the ancient passover became the shortest north-south trading route in the 13th century.

Small geographically but tenacious of spirit, this country has a remarkable story of survival. The early confederation had simple weapons but innate cunning. The people won their first battle by hiding on a high woodland ledge and rolling boulders on to the enemy passing below.

The second battle was won by concentrating a wedge of lances on an enemy encumbered by

BACKGROUND

Eiger and pool:
the beauty of the
Kleine Scheidegg

heavy armour on a sweltering hot day. By outwitting their aggressors the confederates were able to establish their identity against big and powerful neighbours, and in the struggle for freedom there emerged a state jealously guarding its independence and neutrality. Napoleon Bonaparte's ambition to possess the Alpine passes temporarily interrupted the course of Swiss independence. The French invasion lasted for years and the franc was

retained as standard currency. After the fall of
Napoleon, Swiss neutrality, which dates back to
the 16th century, became international law at
the Congress of Vienna in 1815. It is armed
defensive neutrality, with every Swiss male
liable for military service from the age of 20 to
50. As a mark of patriotic trust, to speed up
national mobilisation he keeps his own rifle and
ammunition at home!

The confederation of states became a single
federative state in 1848, with a federal
constitution, since revised and amended. The
Swiss citizen is primarily a member of a
communité (municipality), of which there are
over 3,000, functioning within the structure of
the 23 cantons forming the Swiss
Confederation. Both commune and canton are
self-governing. The Federal Parliament consists
of two legislative chambers, and power at the
top is shared by the seven ministers of the
executive Federal Council.

For one year each minister in rotation is
President of the Confederation, a
representative office through which neither he
nor his family enjoys special favours. The real
power is vested in the people. Major decisions
are subject to referendum and a constitutional
change can be made through a people's
initiative followed by a popular vote. Women,
denied the vote until 1971, are making up for
lost time. The oldest form of democracy still in
action is the open-air parliament,
Landsgemeinde – a genuine public platform.

Neutrality and stability have made Switzerland
a place of refuge for a long influx of exiles. The
humanitarian concept of aid to the suffering is
symbolised by the Swiss flag with colours
reversed adopted by the international Red
Cross. Switzerland is host to over 300
international organisations and many are the
foreign luminaries who have made Switzerland
their home, attracted by the high standard of
living and the reliable Swiss franc – not to
mention the tax benefits.

Switzerland is perhaps one of the few places on
earth where the man or woman in the street still
saves money. Cautious by nature, the Swiss are
also well insured. With a minimal unemployment
rate, they are one of the most hard-working of

nations. But there are too many people and too much expansion. Most of the population of six and a half million is concentrated on the lowland plateau covering three-quarters of the total 15,943 square miles (41,293 sq km); the rest is unproductive land – mountains and lakes. But what price prosperity? Too many demands have been made, and the conservationists are

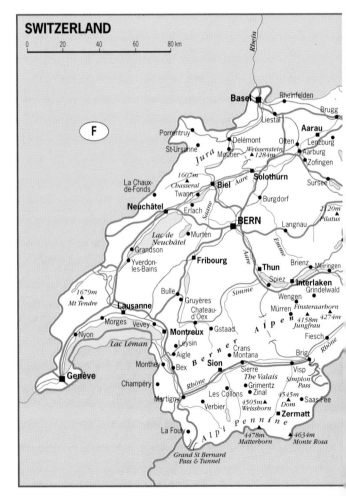

SWITZERLAND

0   20   40   60   80 km

Rhein

Basel
Rheinfelden
Brugg
Liestal
Aarau
Porrentruy
Delémont
Olten
Lenzburg
St-Ursanne
Moutier
Weissenstein ▲1284m
Aarburg
Zofingen
Jura
1607m
Chasseral
Biel
Aare
Solothurn
Sursee
La Chaux-de-Fonds
Twann
Burgdorf
2120m ▲ **Pilatus**
Neuchâtel
Erlach
Saane
BERN
Langnau
Murten
Lac de Neuchâtel
Emme
Grandson
Yverdon-les-Bains
Fribourg
Aare
Thun
Brienz
Meiringen
Spiez
Interlaken
Grindelwald
1679m
Mt Tendre
Bulle
Simme
Wengen
Finsteraarborn
Lausanne
Gruyères
Chateau-d'Oex
Mürren ▲4158m ▲4274m
Jungfrau
A l p e n
Morges
Vevey
Montreux
Gstaad
Fiesch
Lac Léman
Leysin
Crans
Brig
Rhône
Genève
Aigle
Montana
Visp
Monthey
Bex
Sion
B e r n e r
Sierre
The Valais
Simplon Pass
Champéry
Rhône
Grimentz
4545m ▲
Zermatt
Zinal
Saas-Fee
Martigny
Les Collons
4505m ▲
Dom
Verbier
Weissborn
Alpi P e n n i n e
La Fouly
A l p i
4478m ▲
Matterhorn
4634m ▲
Monte Rosa
Grand St Bernard Pass & Tunnel

(F)

understandably worried as survival of the scenic beauty of Switzerland trembles in the balance.

What is causing a dilemma is that tourism is a major factor in the Swiss economy. About a quarter of a million people are directly engaged in tourism, such as in the hotel and catering industry, aerial cable way companies,

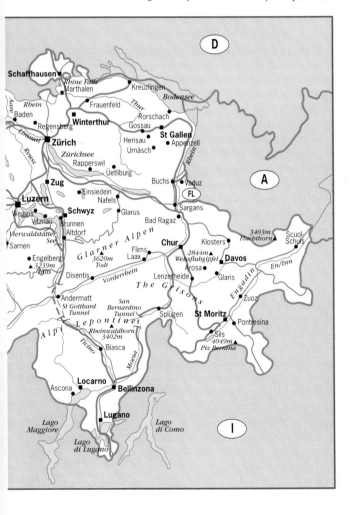

or tourist offices and travel agencies, while half as many again work in branches closely connected with tourism, such as the building trade, the food production industry or the car and transport sector. The gross income from tourism amounts to more than Sfr 20 thousand million, or seven per cent of the Swiss gross national product.

Switzerland needs its visitors, but they threaten to spoil the very thing they come to experience. It was in the first half of the 1800s that the beauty of Switzerland was first discovered by adventurous Britons who spent healthy and invigorating summers in the Alps. In the latter part of the century, however, imaginative Swiss hoteliers sought ways of attracting visitors to enjoy the sun in the magnificent snow-covered landscapes of winter, thus extending the season by several months – and at the same time giving birth to the passion for skiing and winter sports holidays.

Switzerland in Winter

In winter the picturesque mountain villages attract winter sports enthusiasts from all over the world, lured by what is arguably the best skiing in the whole of the Alps. The high altitude of the resorts with the even higher ski areas offers the skier usually reliable snow conditions, and a longer season and more sunshine than most European sports countries. The Jungfrau region has uphill transport to nearly 10,000 feet (3,000m); in St Moritz every run is above 6,000 feet (1,800m); the 'Alpine Metro' in Saas-Fee takes one up to 11,500 feet (3,500m); while at Zermatt it is possible to ski from an incredible 12,750 feet (3,900m).

In addition, the ski areas are situated in some of the most spectacular scenery in the whole of Europe, and the ski pistes are prepared by special machines to ensure excellent conditions for the skier. Twelve cogwheel railways, 47 funiculars and over 500 cableway sections carry tourists up into the heart of the Swiss mountain world. In wintertime about 1,200 skilifts are in operation, and more than 4,000 ski instructors give lessons to 200 ski schools. Splendid facilities also exist for skating, cross-country skiing, ice hockey, curling, tobogganing and

Gondola cars whisk skiers up to the higher slopes from the resorts below

the rapidly growing sport of snowboarding. Winter in Switzerland is not only for the active sports enthusiasts, however. Visitors can enjoy the Alpine air and warm sunshine, take walks along the clearly marked trails in the wonderful settings, be a spectator of the varied sports, or enjoy the delights of picturesque lakeside cities and towns.

Switzerland in Summer

Whether your idea of a perfect holiday is peaceful relaxation, exciting adventure or an escorted tour through ever-changing scenery, Switzerland can satisfy most tastes, with lakeside resorts, Alpine villages, historic towns and modern cities all waiting to be explored.

Seasonal Changes

In the descriptions of the chief towns and resorts in the following pages it should be noted that some of Switzerland's holiday resorts are now more heavily involved in winter as opposed to summer tourism – and vice versa. Consequently, not all the resort facilities detailed are necessarily available year-round; indeed, many hotels and restaurants close for refurbishment once their main season is over, and many of the smaller museums and galleries in the Alpine resorts and villages have limited opening periods. The Swiss National Tourist Office or the information offices of the resorts concerned should be able to advise.

NORTHERN SWITZERLAND

Zürich, the country's biggest
city, is the focal point of German-
speaking Switzerland, which
occupies much of the northern
part of the country. The northeast
borders the Bodensee, fringed
by attractive towns and villages,
while gateway to the strategically-
important northwest is the
fascinating city of Basel, noted
for its carnival and wealth of
monuments and museums.

◆◆◆ (summer)
◆ (winter)
BADEN

The health resort of Baden is
worth visiting even if you are not
interested in 'taking the waters',
since it enjoys a delightful
location in the foothills of the
Jura. Known in Roman times as
Aquae Helveticae, over the
centuries its hot curative sulphur
springs, gushing forth at 48°C
(118°F), have attracted those
seeking relief from rheumatism
and respiratory disorders, and
the resort remains well
equipped with excellent hotels
and pleasant parks, as well as a
casino. Baden's picturesque old
town, the core of the medieval
settlement, contains much of
interest, including a covered
wooden bridge (Holzbrücke)
built in 1810 which leads across
the **River Limmat** to the old
governor's residence, now
housing the **Historical Museum**
containing displays of pottery
from the area, antiques, armour
and excavated coins.
The spa itself is attractively laid
out, with pretty gardens, while
resort facilities include indoor
and outdoor tennis courts, fishing,
and an open air swimming pool.
The Limmat-Promenade along
the river is a pleasant walk.

Hotels

The **Hotel du Parc**, attractively
located between the park and
the thermal baths at Römer
Strasse 24, and the stately
Verenahof/Staadhof, are both
recommended. The **Hirschen** is
cheap and cheerful.

Walks and Excursions

Baden is a good base for walks
and climbs in the **Lagern hills**,
and also for excursions to
Habsburg Castle, about ten
minutes away, which was the
ancestral seat of the Habsburgs,
or, 2 miles (3km) south of Baden,
to the old Cistercian **Abbey of
Wettingen**, which has been
converted into a school for
teachers. Six miles (9km)
northwest of Baden lies **Brugg**,
noteworthy for its bridge and
'back tower' dating from the 11th
century.

Tourist Office: Bahnhofstrasse
50 (tel: (056) 225318)

◆◆◆ (summer)
◆◆◆ (winter)
BASEL (Basle) ✓

This versatile city, the
northwestern gateway to
Switzerland, is a place of
multiple aspects and great
variety. The university, founded
in 1460, is Switzerland's oldest
and perhaps most prestigious,
the numerous museums and art
galleries are known far and
wide, and fascinating old
buildings and a wealth of
monuments lend the city dignity
and charm.

Yet Basel is also a lively, progressive place, a great financial and industrial centre, renowned not only for its attractive stores and boutiques but also for its outstanding research and conference facilities.

More than 500 years ago from 1431 to 1448, the churchmen of Europe assembled at the Ecumenical Council of Basel. Today, scientists and researchers, businessmen and bankers, academics and artists meet here at conferences, seminars and specialist exhibitions. The Swiss Industries Fair alone accounts for over one million visitors a year.

Old Basel's western gateway is the splendid fortified Spalentor

Maybe the people in the frontier city are more outward-looking, more receptive to innovation than most. Sharing some of the characteristics of three nations – Switzerland, Germany and France – they cherish their own way of life. Even the famous *Fasnacht*, or carnival, has its own peculiar quality, as do many other Basel customs. Basel is a modern city, yet has contrived to preserve most of its old town, widely considered one of the finest in Europe. The view of the cathedral from the right bank (**Kleinbasel**) is particularly

NORTHERN SWITZERLAND

impressive, as is that from the **Pfalz** (cathedral promontory) back over Kleinbasel. Then there are the picturesque Gothic sections of town with magnificent fountains, the market square in front of the imposing **Rahtaus** (town hall) and the **Spalentor**, the city's western gateway and reputedly the most beautiful in Switzerland.

Places of Interest

Basel's rich, extensive range of museums houses some of the world's most prestigious collections of old and new masterpieces. Within easy walking distance are more than 30 lively and interesting museums.

Kunstmuseum (Museum of Fine Arts), St Alban-Graben 16. This is the pride and joy of Basel's museums and said to be the oldest public art collection in the world, dating from 1662. It is rich in old masters such as Witz, the Holbeins, Grünewald and Manuel as well as great collections of 19th- and 20th-century art.
Open: daily except Mondays.

Museum für Gegenwartskunst (Museum of Contemporary Art), St Alban Rheinweg 60. Widely recognised as Europe's leading museum of art of the 1960s, 1970s and 1980s, it features such artists as Frank Stella, Donald Judd, Bruce Nauman, Richard Long and Jonathan Borofsky.
Open: daily except Mondays.

Historisches Museum, Barfüsserkirche, Barfüsserplatz. A 14th-century Franciscan church has been transformed into a historical museum housing the cathedral treasures, riches of the Basel guilds. Gothic sculptures and tapestries.
Open: daily except Tuesdays.

Monuments: Basel's other fine monuments include the **Münster** (Cathedral), founded in 1019 by the Emperor Henry II; the **Predigerkirche** or **Dominican Church** (1269); the **Rathaus** (town hall) of 1504–14; and town mansions and corporate houses from the 15th and 16th centuries.

Tierpark (Zoo). Here, some 4,000 animals and 600 different species live in a magnificent park in the middle of the city. A special part of the zoo is put aside for children.

Guided sightseeing tours by coach, depart daily from the Hotel Victoria (near the railway station SBB) at 10.00hrs. Also, accompanied walks through the old city and excursions to the countryside around Basel are organised by the Basel Tourist Board from May to October.

Basel Carnival

There can be remarkably few annual revelries that start at the ungodly hour of 04.00 hours, especially on a chilly Monday in February or early March. The Basler *Fasnacht* is one of them. Not content with that, it lasts for three days and three whole nights, which is enough for anyone to warm up and let off steam… The *Fasnacht*, described by locals as the best free show of the year', begins on the Monday following Ash Wednesday.

The musicians' fantastic masks and costumes set the tone for Basel's three-day madness at **Fasnacht'**

Numerous carnival associations parade through the narrow streets of the old town. Wearing grotesque masks and with small lanterns perched on their heads, come pipers and drummers, holding huge transparent lanterns with the emblem of their particular association in caricature. This curious parade lasts until dawn. On Monday and Wednesday afternoons the associations, or *cliques* as they are known, with their fifes and drums, again march through the streets.

On the Tuesday the carnival lanterns are exhibited at the Basler Halle, which normally houses part of the Swiss Industries Fair. The exhibition is well worth a visit, for many of the lanterns are real works of art, designed by the best local artists.

Events of the Wednesday, the third and last day of the *Fasnacht*, are similar to those of Monday but without the opening ceremony. The fun reaches its climax in the evening and lasts until the early hours of Thursday morning, when Basel goes back to work again… and starts looking forward to next year's carnival!

Hotels

The de luxe class **Drei Könige Hotel** at Blumenrain 8, which flanks the Rhein and is only five minutes from the market place, is excellent; also the moderately

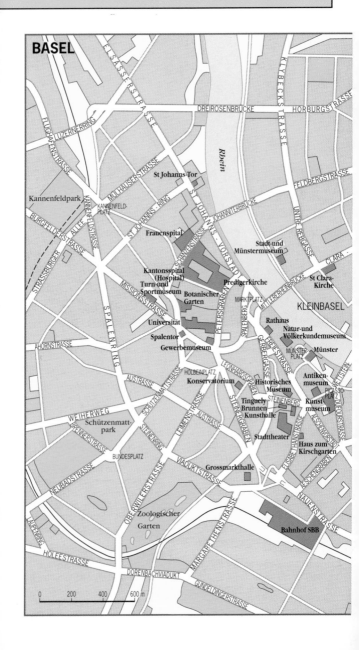

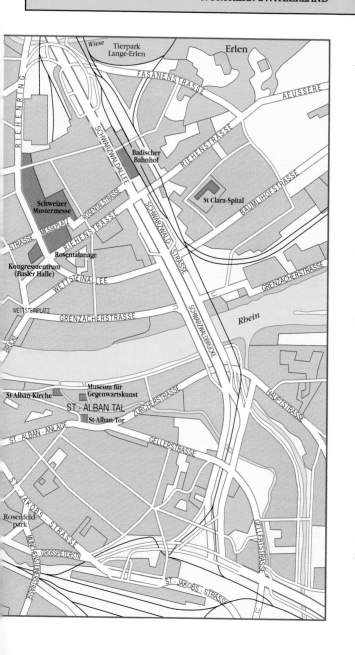

priced riverside **Kraft am Rhein Hotel** at Rheingasse 2. Try also **The Temfelhof** for real decorative character.

Entertainment

One of the most popular places for an evening drink is the **Campari Bar** in the Kunsthalle Garde, facing the famous Tinguely Fountain. Try too the stylish bar in the **Hotel Euler**, and for live loud music the **Café Atlantis** in Klosterberg.

Restaurants

One of the best in the city is **La Rotisserie des Rois** in the **Drei Konige Hotel**, which has a wonderful atmosphere and serves excellent food. Also recommended is the **Schnoggeloch at the Kraft Hotel**, which in summer occupies a terrace on the riverbank.

Shopping

The fashionable shopping street of Basel is the Freie Strasse, leading to the marketplace and town hall. And the fleamarket, on Saturdays at Petersplatz, is a popular hunting ground for the curio-lovers.

Excursions

A popular excursion from Basel is to **Augusta Raurica**, the site of a Roman colony founded in 27BC. Of particular interest are the theatre and the remains of several temples, as well as the museum located within a reconstruction of a Roman house. Basel is also a good base for exploring other regions and villages of northwest Switzerland, many of them with old castles, such as

Lenzburg. Likewise the towns of **Aarau**, **Aarburg** and **Zofingen** all have a rich historic past and are well worth visiting. Around **Liestal** the countryside is delightful in spring, when thousands of cherry trees break into blossom.

Tourist Office: Blumenrain 2, CH-4001 Basel (tel: 061-2615050)

◆◆◆ (summer)
◆ (winter)
SCHAFFHAUSEN ✓

Capital of Switzerland's northernmost canton, Schaffhausen, wonderfully set on terrraces on the right bank of the Rhein, contains some of the country's most impressive ancient buildings. The majority of these 16th- to 18th-century buildings – richly embellished with statues, reliefs, frescos and oriel windows - are found in the old town centre, which is a pedestrian-only zone. Particularly impressive are the late Renaissance frescos on the **Haus zum Ritter** (Knight's House) and the richly decorated façade of the **Haus zum Goldenen Ochsen** (Golden Ox). In the public squares are historic fountains, and no fewer than 12 guildhalls, some now restaurants, attest to the prosperity of their masters. The ancient heart of the town was the street market, located in what is now the Vordergasse. Presiding over all is St John's church, noted for its excellent acoustics. Music-lovers continue to delight in its Good Friday concerts as well as the Bach Festival held every three years.

A fine view of the Rhein is had from Schaffhausen's Munot Fortress

Places of Interest

Museum zu Allerheiligen (All Saints' Museum). Its rooms contain a notable cultural and historical collection, including prehistoric collections from local excavations. Virtually all the manuscripts of the former Benedictine library are preserved in the city library located in the old granary (Kornhaus) of the cloister complex. *Open:* daily except Mondays.

Münster (All Saints' Church). This 11th-century church built of yellow ochre coloured stone is one of the best examples of Romanesque architecture in Switzerland, and today houses a school of music. In the adjoining medieval herb garden the various plants and seedlings are identified in careful script.

Munot Fortress. Superb views of the town and its surroundings can be enjoyed from the Munot Fortress which overlooks Schaffhausen. The top of the fortress is reached by climbing a spiral ramp inside the keep. It was built between 1564 and 1585 and the watchman and his family still live in the tower. Every evening at 21.00 hours he rings the bell – once the signal to close the town gates and public houses.

Rheinfall. Nearby Neuhausen contains what are said to be the most powerful waterfalls in Europe – the Rheinfall (Falls of the Rhein), with a height of 75 feet (23m). On a platform extending over a part of the basin, spectators can experience the water thundering beneath their feet and swirling around them. For the truly courageous there is even a small boat which goes to the rock formation at the foot of the falls. The spectacle is best seen during high water in summer, in July particularly.

Hotels and Restaurants

The **Hotel Parkvilla** at Parkstrasse 18 is elegantly furnished and stylish, while the **Bellevue** has an attractive terrace. The **Rheinhotel Fischerzunft** enjoys an excellent reputation for cuisine.
Tourist Office: **Fronwagturm 12**, CH-8201 Schaffhausen (tel; (053) 255141)

The seething rush of the mighty Rheinfall near Schaffhausen

◆◆◆ (summer)
◆◆ (winter)
SOLOTHURN ✓

Solothurn's reputation as Switzerland's best-preserved and most beautiful baroque town is well earned. One of the oldest towns north of the Alps, its name is of Celtic origin, and the Romans built a fort there, traces of which can still be seen.
In this small area, the visitor can study sacred buildings of European importance such as the 17th-century **Jesuitenkirche** (Jesuits' Church) or the 18th-century **St Ursenkathedrale** (Cathedral of St Ursus), as well as the seats of patrician families, charming burghers' houses, forbidding military defences, of which the **Krummeturm** (Twisted Tower) is the most striking feature, and beautiful old fountains.

Museums

The **Kunstmuseum** (Museum of Fine Art) has an impressive collection of post-1850 Swiss art and old masters.
Open: daily except Mondays.
The **Naturmuseum** (Natural History Museum) is a joy for children to visit, as they may both see and touch the exhibits.
Open: daily except Mondays.
One of Europe's largest collections of weapons is to be seen in the **Altes Zeughaus** (old Arsenal Museum).
Open: daily except Mondays; weekday mornings in winter.
The **Historisches Museum Blumenstein** (just outside the town centre) shows how the ruling classses lived.
Open: daily except Mondays.

Sport

For sports enthusiasts there are facilities for tennis, squash, riding, swimming and miniature golf in the town and its immediate surroundings. In summer, the **Weissenstein/Balmberg** area is ideal for walks and hikes, and in winter there is skiing, cross-country skiing as well as tobogganing.

Hotels

The **Krone (Couronne)** at Hauptgasse 64, one of the oldest inns in Switzerland, is the best hotel in town. A little less expensive, the **Roter Turm/Tour Rouge**, has a bowling alley.

Restaurants

The **Zunfthaus zu Wirthen**, situated in the old town guildhouse at Hauptgasse 41,
serves seasonal dishes made from fresh local produce. **Chez Derron**, Hauptgasse 79, is a restaurant/grill that enjoys a fine reputation in historic surroundings. The **Tiger**, stalen 35, has a pleasant terrace.

Excursions

Numerous excursions are possible in the immediate vicinity, such as to the **hermitage in the Verena gorge**; to the oldest and most important **stork settlement** in Switzerland, in Altreu; and to Solothurn's 'local' mountain, the **Weissenstein** whose peak – reached by chairlift – offers an incomparable view across the swiss Mittelland to the snow-covered Alpine chain.
The Lake of Biel (Bieler See), the Bernese Oberland, Central Switzerland, Bern, Basel, Luzern, Zürich and Neuchâtel are all within easy reach.

Tourist Office: Kronenplatz, CH-4500 Solothurn (tel: (065) 221924)

◆◆◆ (summer)
◆◆◆ (winter)
ZÜRICH

Although Switzerland's largest city is small by world standards, with a population of around 400,000, it nevertheless boasts all the advantages of an international metropolis, together with an attractive location at the northern end of Lake Zürich (Zürichsee). Switzerland's most important centre of commerce, banking and industry – silk, cotton, machinery, paper and food – Zürich is also a main cultural centre of German-speaking Switzerland.

Sightseeing

Walking is the best way to get to know the attractive old town. The **Lindenhof** is a good starting point and ofers an attractive view over the old town. In 15BC the Romans built a customs post here, thereby founding Turicum, now known as Zürich. However, Zürich was not recorded as a town in official documents until the year 929. In 1336 aritsans organised in guilds took over the government of the city; nowadays these guilds appear in public just once a year, on the third Monday in April, when the spring festival known as *Sechseläuten* is held. Clad in traditional guild costumes, the men parade around the city, arriving at **Sechseläutenplatz** towards evening. In a show almost medieval in character, a cotton-wool snowman symbolising winter is burnt on a giant bonfire, while bands of guild horsemen gallop around his place of execution.

The modern city silhouette is dominated by the striking towers and spires of three old churches – the **Grossmünster**, endowed by Charlemagne; **St Peterskirche**, which boasts Europe's largest clock face (28½ feet/8.6 metres), and the **Fraumünster**, greatly admired for its stained-glass windows by Marc Chagall (completed 1970). An important milestone in Zürich's development into an important international financial, economic and trade centre was the foundation of the Zürich Stock Exchange (**Börse**) in 1877, now the world's fourth most important.

Hotels

The **Baur au Lac Hotel**, Talstrasse 1, with its lovely garden, superb restaurant and high standards, is one of the best hotels in Switzerland. Also first-rate are the **Savoy Hotel Baur en Ville**, Am Paradeplatz, the **Dolder Grand Hotel**, Kurhausstrasse 20, – a grand hotel in all senses of the word – and the **Eden au Lac**, Utoquai 45. Of the moderately priced establishments the family run **Hotel Leonhard**, Limmatquai, enjoys an excellent reputation, as does the budget-priced **Hotel Bristol**, Stampfenbachstrasse 34.

Culture and Entertainment

There are more than 30 museums in **Zürich** with a great variety of exhibitions. The many interesting works of art in the **Schweizerisches Landesmuseum** (Swiss National Museum) opposite the railway station, for example, provide a lively demonstration of Swiss history.

Open: daily except Mondays.

The municipal theatre (**Schauspielhaus**), the Opera House (**Opernhaus**), the Concert Hall (**Tonhalle**) and various smaller theatres as well as other institutes offer a varied selection of cultural events. Culture is highlighted in the annual June Festival, whose chief characteristics are concerts, opera, ballet, drama, exhibitions, and lectures all centring on a particular theme. Full details of events in the city appear in the *Zürich Weekly Bulletin*.

The twin towers of the Grossmünster watch over Zürich's river, the Limmat

Located a taxi-ride from Zürich's city centre, in Zollikerstrasse, the **Emil Bührle Collection** is an impressive collection of French paintings, particularly of the 19th century, including works by Corot, Courbet and Delacroix and Impressionist paintings by Cézanne, Degas, Gauguin, Manet, Renoir and Van Gogh. Unfortunately, there are very limited opening hours, so before making the visit, check the times in advance with the tourist office.

For those in search of nightlife, night-clubs are numerous and range from the fashionable to the folkish.

Restaurants

At the upper end of the price range the **Agnes Amberg**, Hottingerstrasse 5, and the famous **Kronenhalle** are both outstanding. Of the less expensive restaurants, the huge old **Zeughamskeller**, Am Paradeplatz, has its devotees, as does the locals' favourite, **Bierhalle Kropf**, nearby. For pastries and atmosphere, the **Schober**, in Napfgasse, is a 'must'.

Shopping

Zürich's international reputation also rests on its excellent shopping facilities and its fame

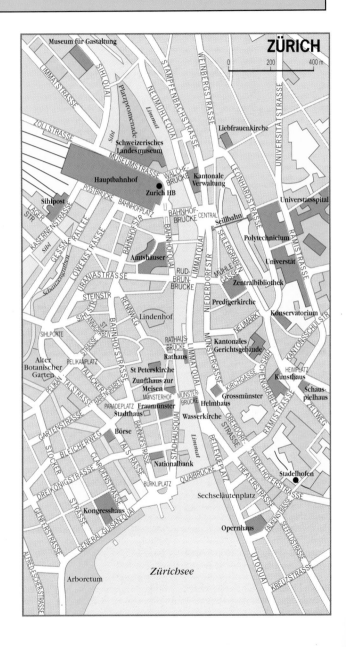

ZÜRICH

0   200   400 m

Museum für Gastaltung

Liebfrauenkirche

LIMMAT STRASSE

SIHLQUAI

Platzpromenade

NEUMÜHLEQUAI

 S TAMPFENBACHSTRASSE

WEINBERGSTRASSE

UNIVERSITÄT STRASSE

ZOLLSTRASSE

Limmat

Sihl

Schweizerisches
Landesmuseum

MUSEUMSTRASSE

WALCHE-
BRÜCKE

Kantonale
Verwaltung

LEONHARDSTRASSE

Hauptbahnhof

Zurich HB

BAHNHOF-
BRÜCKE CENTRAL

Universtatsspital

Sihlpost

POSTBRÜCKE

BAHNHOFPLATZ

Seilbahn

RÄMISTRASSE

LÄGER
STR

KASERNENSTRASSE

SIHL

BAHNHOFSTR

BAHNHOFQUAI

SEILERGRABEN

Polytechnicum

GESSNE RALLEE

LÖWENSTRASSE

Amtshäuser

LIMMATQUAI

MÜHLE
GASSE

Universtät

Schanzengraben

URANIASTRASSE

RUD.-
BRUN-
BRÜCKE

NIEDERDORFSTR

Zentralbibliothek

STEINSTR

RENNWEG

Lindenhof

Predigerkirche

Konservatorium

SIHLPORTE

SIHL

SIHLAMTGRABEN

STR

BAHNHOFSTRASSE

RATHAUS-
BRÜCKE

NEUMARKT

KANTONSSCHULSTR

Alter
Botanischer
Garten

PELIKANPLATZ

Rathaus

MÜNSTERGASSE

Kantonales
Gerichtsgebäude

HIRSCHENGRABEN

HEIMPLATZ

Kunsthaus

PELIKAN

TALACKER

BÄRENGASSE

St Peterskirche

KIRCHGASSE

RÄMISTRASSE

Schaus-
pielhaus

TALSTRASSE

Zunfthaus zur
Meisen

Grossmünster

ZELTWEG

MÜNSTERHOF

MÜNSTER-
BRÜCKE

Helmhaus

OBERDORF

PARADEPLATZ

Fraumünster

STRASSE

STADELHOFERSTRASSE

GARTENSTRASSE

Stadthaus

Wasserkirche

BELLEVUEPLATZ

THEATERSTRASSE

Börse

BAHNHOFSTRASSE

STADTHAUSQUAI

Limmat

STOCKER

BLEICHERWEG

CLARIDENSTRASSE

Nationalbank

Stadelhofen

DREIKONIGSTRASSE

TALSTRASSE

BURKLIPLATZ

QUAIBRÜCKE

FALKENSTRASSE

STRASSE

GENERAL GUISANQUAI

Sechseläutenplatz

SEEFELDQUAI

GENFERSTRASSE

Kongresshaus

Opernhaus

UTOQUAI

ALFRED-ESCHERSTRASSE

Zürichsee

KREUZSTRASSE

Arboretum

as an art dealing centre – a number of notable auction houses are based here.
With its elegant boutiques and famous *couturières* the **Bahnhofstrasse** is considered one of the most attractive shopping streets in the world, the unusual distinction of having a catacomb of bank vaults beneath it.

Excursions

Only 15 minutes from Zürich via the expressway leading beyond the airport lies the industrial city of **Winterthur**, noted for its impressive art collections, particularly those displayed in the **Oskar Reinhart Foundation** in Stadthausstrasse and in the villa in which the benefactor

used to live in Am Romerholz. Among the paintings on display are priceless works by Brueghel, Cézanne and Van Gogh.
Open: daily except Mondays.
Other popular excursions are to **Üetliburg**, the most northern peak in the Albis ridge; the medieval village of **Regensberg**, with its half-timbered houses and imposing castle; and **Rapperswil**, known as 'the town of roses'.

Tourist Office: Bahnhofplatz 15, CH-8023 Zürich (tel: (01) 2114000)

A tram in Zürich's Bahnhofstrasse; this elegant street is car-free, enhancing the pleasure of shopping

CENTRAL SWITZERLAND

CENTRAL SWITZERLAND

This part of the country has been luring discerning travellers since long before the current fascination with skiing and winter sports. Byron, Shelley, Longfellow, Medelssohn, Wagner and Brahms are just a few of the many famous names who have been inspired by this delightful region, which offers much in the way of interest, not least the splendid town of Luzern and the richly varied canton of Bern. To the south lies the Bernese Oberland, with its spectacular mountains, glaciers,

The Swiss capital, Bern: the country's tallest spire dominates the old town

waterfalls and lakes, plus pretty villages and holiday resorts.

◆◆ (summer)
◆◆◆ (winter)
BEATENBERG
Lying in the heart of the Swiss Alps at an altitude of 3,773 feet (1,150m), Beatenberg is one of the leading holiday resorts in the Bernese Oberland, universally popular thanks to numerous natural attractions that include its fine location, mild

climate, unrivalled view of the entire Alpine chain, and a particularly sunny situation. Beatenberg offers some 3,500 beds in hotels, inns, chalets, rented apartments and health homes that nestle among fir trees. Beneath the village lie the famous St Beatus's Caves (Beatus Höhlen).

Summer attractions include hiking paths, mini-golf, tennis and other sporting activities, and a wide-ranging programme of entertainment and excursions.

Excursion

For an unrivalled view of Beatenberg and the Alpine chain go to the top of **Niederhorn**, which is reached by chairlift. At an altitude of 6,397 feet (1,950m) there are spectacular views from viewing platforms at the top, south over Beatenberg and beyond Lake Thun to the glaciers of the Jungfrau Massif. To the southwest, Mont Blanc is just visible in the distance.

Tourist Office: CH-3803 Beatenberg (tel: (036) 411286)

◆◆◆ (summer)
◆◆◆ (winter)
BERN (BERNE) ✓

By European standards, Bern – the capital of Switzerland – is not a big city. It has only 140,000 inhabitants, or 300,000 if you count those in the suburbs, but it is very Swiss, very Alemanic, very picturesque and very romantic.

The city was founded a century before the Swiss Confederation itself, by the last Duke of Zähringen, Berchtold V, for

strategic reasons. The duke entrusted one of his noblemen, Cuno von Budenberg, with the task of building a city there. The city was started in 1191 on the site of Nydegg Castle. Cuno built a city wall, in the centre of which rose a great Clock Tower, and in it was the main gate. In front of the city wall is a natural hollow which served as a moat. In the 13th century, under the protectorate of Count Peter of Savoy, the city's frontier was extended westwards and a new city wall, with the prison tower as its main gateway, was erected. In the 14th century there were further additions to the city, taking it to where the main station now stands.

In 1405 the greater part of the town was destroyed by fire. The houses were rebuilt on the old foundations, but instead of wood, sandstone from nearby quarries was used as building material. Most of these houses were replaced in the 16th and 17th centuries by new buildings whose harmonious appearance and richness of detail are a delight.

Bern's greatest territorial power was reached between the years 1536 and 1798, mostly gained at the cost of the House of Savoy. Large territories along Lac Léman (the Lake of Geneva) came under Bernese rule and it is chiefly thanks to Bern that much of the French part of Switzerland is today within the Confederation.

The invasion of the French in 1798 destroyed Bern's position of authority. However, it became the cantonal capital and in 1848 had the honour of being chosen

CENTRAL SWITZERLAND

by the first Swiss parliament as the capital of the Swiss Federation.

In the past fifty years Bern has expanded enormously, and wide bridges now span the Aare to link the old city with its new suburbs. While retaining its medieval appearance, the old city (Nydegg) has developed into an important business centre.

Happily sited where German-speaking Switzerland meets French, Bern has a distinct touch of the latter. A breath of Gallic spirit permeates its streets and its unostentatious baroque buildings while, in the arcades, rapid-fire French mingles with the ponderous tones of the Bern-German dialect.

City Features

Arcades. Characteristic of Bern's streets are the medieval arcades let into the façades of the buildings. Even in the worst of weathers you can walk from one end of the city to the other without getting your feet wet. The people of Bern call it *lauben* ('arcading') when they stroll through these airy vaults which open into the roadway in

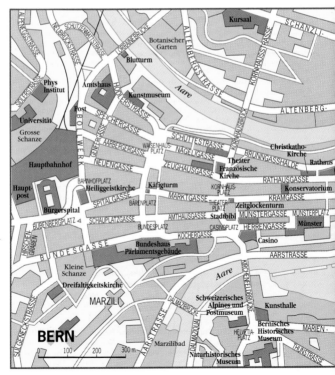

sweeping arches, while the other side is flooded with light from the stores and window displays in Europe's first and largest sheltered shopping area. The city guards its arcades with a jealous eye; no house may be rebuilt or renovated without an arcade on the ground floor, and every façade has to fit in with neighbouring ones.

Cathedral and Town Hall. High above the rooftops towers the Münster (Cathedral of St Vincent), one of the finest ecclesiastical buildings in Switzerland. Like most of Bern it dates from the 15th century.

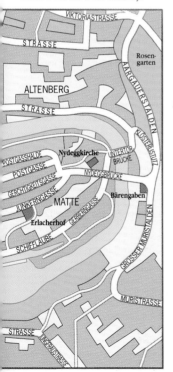

Only a few years after the fire of 1405, work began on a new town hall. Broad and solid, this Gothic building, restored to all its old splendour, stands between Rathausgasse and Postgasse. Then, five years after its completion, the citizens of Bern set about building a new cathedral. A memorial tablet gives the year the foundation stone was laid as 1421. The cathedral dominates the curve of the Aare, where the steep ramparts of the old walls plunge down to the river.

Clock Tower. The Zeitglockenturm is one of Bern's most popular attractions. Originally dating from the 12th century, it was gutted in 1405, and was rebuilt in stone. In 1530 the astronomical or calendar clock, showing the position of the sun, moon, stars and planets as well as the month and day of the week, was constructed; and at the same time the delightful mechanical figure-play was made. This includes a jester, a parade of marching bears, a cock, a knight in golden armour and Father Time.

Fountains. Below the Cathedral is Junkerngasse where the houses of the old city aristocracy stand in four-square comfort. Rathausgasse and Postgasse,which broaden out virtually into extended squares, and Kramgasse and Gerechtigkeitsgasse, with their magnificent 16th-century fountains, each with a theme, run parallel to it.

Market. Spread along streets and squares, this extends as far as the Bundesplatz, where the merry bustle surges up against the somewhat formal Swiss parliament building.

New town

The new town, across the Aare, is accessible by four bridges. Of special interest here is the **Bundeshaus** (Federal Palace), a domed 19th-century Florentine Renaisssance-style building. Also in the new town, the **Schweizerisches Alpines Museum** (Swiss Alpine Museum) highlights the natural history and culture of the Swiss Alps, including the history of mountaineering. The **Schweizerisches Postmuseum** (Swiss Postal Museum) displays items from the history of postal and communication services in Switzerland plus a collection of stamps from around the world. The two museums are situated together at Helvetiaplatz 4. *Open*: daily.

The extraordinary mock 16th-century building of the **Bernisches Historisches Museum** (Bernese Historical Museum) at Helvetiaplatz 5 is really less than a century old. *Open*: daily except Mondays; free Sundays.

Close by, at Bernastrasse 15, the collections of the **Natur-historisches Museum** (Natural History Museum) figure among the world's richest. *Open*: daily. Free Wednesday, Saturday and Sunday afternoons.

Hotels

The **Schweizerhof**, Bahnhofplatz 11, is one of Switzerland's finest hotels, with a well-deserved reputation for the standards of accommodation, service and food. Another luxury hotel is the **Bellevue Palace**, Kochergasse

3–5, while less expensive but hugely characterful is the **Goldener Schlüssel**, Rathausgasse 72.

Entertainment

Bern has a regular opera and theatre season running from late September to April. Opera and ballet are presented at the **Stadttheater** and concerts at a number of other halls. Plays are usually in German. Full details of productions are available from local tourist offices.

Restaurants

The **Schultheissenstube** at the **Schweizerhof Hotel** is expensive but generally well worth it, and also highly recommended is the very formal **Bellevue Grill** in the **Bellevue Palace Hotel**. In the moderately priced category **Ratskeller**, Gerechtigkeitsgasse 81, is very popular.

Excursions

Popular excursions are to the district of **Emmental**, about ten minutes away, and noted for its cheese; and to the ancient celtic city of **Thun**, which lies southeast of Bern, on Lake Thun (Thuner See), a summer playground for waterskiers and the yachting set. Other areas worth visiting are **Schwarzenburg** and **Seeland**, and the villages lying on the shores of Seeland Lake (Bieler See) such as **Twann**, **Ligerz** and **Erlach**.

Tourist Office: Im Hauptbahnhof, Bahnhofplatz, CH-3001 Bern (tel: (031) 227676)

◆◆◆ (summer)
◆◆ (winter)
BRIENZ
Nestling between the upper end of lake Brienz (Brienzer See) and

the Southern slopes of the Brienzer Rothorn, Brienz is located nine miles (15km) east of Interlaken in the very heart of Switzerland. At 1,863 feet (568m) above sea-level it enjoys a mild mountain climate thanks to the compensating effects of the lake. It is well known for its local craft of wood-carving.

From the Brunngasse up to the old church, the village centre has been well preserved, its wooden houses in the narrow alleys ablaze with pelargoniums in the summer, while the

Brienz is a popular summer resort

lakeshore promenade is among the village's many delights. The lake itself is available for swimming, waterskiing, sailing, surfing or fishing, while a trip on one of its famous paddle-steamers is a delightful diversion.

An extensive network of marked paths around the village and up into the mountains makes it easy for visitors to explore the resort's surroundings, including the neighbouring villages of

Schwanden, Hofstetten and Brienzwiler.

Brienzer Rothorn Bahn

The famous steam-driven rack railway takes visitors to the top of the Brienzer Rothorn. Construction was started in 1890 and in 1891 the first engine took one hour to cover the distance of 4.7 miles (7.6km) with an average incline of 22° to the 7.710ft (2,350m) peak. Seven steam engines are in service every summer from June to October; five of them date back to 1891/92, the others to 1933 and 1936. The trip – offering panoramic views – is unforgettable. To reach the summit from the terminus there is a 15- to 20-minute walk. The Rothorn itself is the starting point for many good walks, but visitors wishing to enjoy a spectacular sunset or sunrise are advised to book a bed in the **Rothorn Kulm** mountain hotel well in advance.

Hotels

Brienz offers a range of comfortable, traditional hotels with some 500 beds, as well as apartments, a youth hostel, and camping sites. The **Hotel Bären**, which borders the lake and has its own private beach, has a pleasant garden and terrace, as well as a swimming pool. The smaller **Hotel Schönegg** is also recommended.

Excursions

The **Axalp** lies about six miles (10km) from Brienz and can be reached by public transport, car or special excursions in the season. At some 5,250 feet (1,600m) above sea-level, it is popular in summer for relaxing, touring and walking, while overnight accommodation is available in two hotels and a tourist hostel.

Ballenberg Open Air Museum of rural dwellings and lifestyle, just northeast of Brienz, can be reached by public transport, but travel companies put on special excursion buses in the season. Here examples of houses and settlements from all parts of Switzerland have been reconstructed in an impressive park comprising of seven theme areas.

The museum was opened in 1978 with 15 completed houses. Now, more than 50 buildings from various parts of Switzerland are open to the public, and it is planned to reconstruct a total of 100 buildings. People employed in traditional crafts such as bread-baking, cheese-making, basket-weaving, spinning, weaving, and wood-carving bring the old houses to life. *Open*: daily from mid-April to late October.

Tourist Office: Beim Bahnhof, CH-3855 Brienz (tel: (036) 513242)

◆◆◆ (summer)
◆ (winter)

BRUNNEN

Located on the shores of Lake Luzern (Vierwaldstätter See) and framed by mountains, Brunnen is a resort with characteristic Swiss houses and shops and a lakeside promenade complete with attractive cafés.

Visitors should look out for the gaily painted water pumps dotted around the village, and be sure to visit the pretty little chapel in the centre of town. Brunnen lies at the head of Lake Uri (Urnersee), the most dramatic branch of Lake Luzern, its sheer cliffs plummeting into the deep waters which here give it the appearance of a Norwegian fjord.

Lake Luzern itself offers a variety of activities. Steamers leaving from Brunnen call at historic sites on the lake such as William Tell's chapel and the Rütli meadow, birthplace of the Swiss Confederation.

Nearby **Flüelen** is a watersports paradise with waterskiing, sailing and windsurfing, while Brunnen itself has a lido where you can bathe in the lake or swim in the indoor pool.

Sports facilities in the resort include mountain bikes, bicycles, bowling, tennis and table tennis. A fitness trail in the woods is a fun activity to try, or you can take the train to **Seedorf** for an afternoon's horse-riding. Children might enjoy the play area on the lakeside, where there are small animals to stroke and photograph.

Hotels
Recommended hotels include the **Bellevue au Lac Kursaal**, an elegant establishment situated on the lakeside promenade, with magnificent views of the lakes and mountains; and the **Cabana**, not far from the Urmiberg cable car with its panoramic views and possibilities for walking.

Entertainment
For evening entertainment, cruises with music and dancing are very popular, or you can try your luck in the casino. Live bands perform throughout the summer, and every week a Swiss folklore evening is held with Alpine music. The bars in

Visitors enjoy strolling along the lakeshore promenade at Brunnen

Brunnen have a Continental atmosphere, and for variety you can sample a cheese fondue or pizza.

Tourist Office: Bahnhofstrasse 32, CH-6440 Brunnen (tel: (043) 311777)

◆◆◆ (summer)
◆◆◆ (winter)
ENGELBERG
Dominated by a 12th-century Benedictine monastery, this pretty village is set at the foot of the Titlis mountains at the heart of a beautiful valley that leads up from Lake Luzern (Vierwaldstätter See). It is a charming spot with a relaxed atmosphere.

The Titlis Glacier means that it can boast snow year-round – you can usually even enjoy limited skiing here in July! There are over 35 miles (56km) of downhill runs in three areas, with something for all grades of skier. The run from Titlis to the village is about eight miles (13km) long.

A free ski-bus service takes about three minutes to transport you from the village to the new gondola cable car that takes you up to **Gerschnialp** at 4,100 feet (1,250m), from where two further cable cars run parallel up to **Trubsee** at 6,000 feet (1,800m).

From Trubsee a two-stage cable car rises to nearly 10,000 feet (3000 metres). The second stage has the novelty of the world's first rotating cabin, allowing thrilling views of the dramatic glacial scenery.

Many of Engelberg's walking paths are close to the ski areas,

so that non-skiers can meet up with family or friends at lunchtime.

The village has a good range of additional facilities, such as indoor skating and curling rinks, two tennis courts, swimming pools, tea rooms and plenty of excursions, as well as guided tours of the monastery, making it a popular resort during the summer too.

Restaurants and Entertainment
In the winter season there are après-ski get-togethers at several hotels, while every Tuesday there is a horse sleigh ride through the village followed by a fondue party. For some typical folklore try the **Bänklialp Hotel** or the restaurant **Sporthalle** where there is also a bowling alley. Engelberg has some delightful little restaurants and plenty of *Stüblis* and bars – the bar of the **Hotel Hess** is a popular meeting place and there is music and dancing at the **Carmena**, **Spindle**, **Einwäldi** and **Bierlialp**. The casino has a gaming room and night spot with dancing. The **Dorint-Hotel Regina Titlis**, in the centre of town in Dorfstrasse, has a swimming pool and sauna.

Tourist Office: Klosterstrasse 3, CH-6390 Engelberg (tel: (041) 941161)

◆◆◆ (summer)
◆◆◆ (winter)
GRINDELWALD
Popularly known as the 'village of the glaciers', Grindelwald is situated at the foot of the north face of the Eiger on a broad,

The Wetterhorn broods over Grindelwald, with its typical Alpine church

sunny plateau some 3,500 feet (1,050m) above sea-level. The most famous and largest ski resort in the Bernese Oberland, the town is a gateway to the whole Jungfrau region with its enormous choice for intermediate and advanced skiers.

There are three main areas for good skiing. **First** is reached by chairlift from the centre of the village. **Kleine Scheidegg** by mountain railway from the station, and **Männlichen** by gondolaway which starts about five minutes by road from the centre.

In winter Grindelwald is an excellent choice for both skiers and non-skiers, but as it is the only resort in the region accessible by car, it can be very busy in peak season. Visitors should also consider carefully which ski pass to buy as there are big differences in price and validity.

Mountaineering

Grindelwald is excellent for mountaineers. The Grindelwald mountain guides have their own climbing centre which not only

Skiing at over 6,700 feet (2,000m) near the Kleine Scheidegg in the Bernese Oberland

offers training in rock climbing and on ice but also one- or two-day tours to the various Bernese Oberland peaks, glacier hiking and climbing weeks and, in addition, walking and hiking for senior citizens and trekking in the Alpine foothills.

Sports Facilities

For tennis fans there are 11 open air courts; and the sports centre's ice rink, open for skating from July to April, is also used for tennis in May and June.

The sports centre, centrally located, also offers a sauna and solarium, fitness facilities, table tennis, a children's play area, a casino, and an indoor pool. Those who prefer swimming in the sun can walk up to the Hellbach open-air pool in **Grund**, while there is a marked fitness trail for training purposes and two Alpine orienteering routes.

Courses

Those who want to look down

on the world can attend weekend courses in hang-gliding or para-gliding, while those more attracted by Alpine flora can learn more about it along the **Grütli-Waldlehrpfad**. The Heimatmuseum offers information on Grindelwald customs, the beginning of mountaineering and winter sports, and on Alpine dairies and cheese-making.

Hotels

There is a wide choice of accommodation in the resort, including modern hotels with indoor pools and bars, second and third category hotels. family-run guest houses, charming wooden chalets and holiday apartments – more than 8,000 beds in total. The five-star **Grand Hotel Regina** has an enviable position in the village and its gardens, heated outdoor pool and sun terrace enjoy one of the most glorious Alpine backdrops imaginable.

The **Hotel Belvedere** is a first-class establishment offering high standards of service and cuisine in a lovely setting. The **Fiescherblick** is a modern mountain inn offering good value and excellent local knowledge.

Entertainment

The **Spider Club** is a lively music venue for arachnophiles, while **Herby's Bar** offers a more sophisticated atmosphere.

Restaurants

The best restaurant in town is almost certainly the **Jagerstube** at the **Regina** – it is stylish and serves delicious food. The **Alte Post** combines superb Alpine atmosphere with fine local cuisine.

Excursions

There is a post coach to **Meiringen** and **Rosenlaui** via the Grosse Scheidegg and the Schwarzwaldalp; Europe's most scenic gondola takes only half an hour to reach **First**, a difference in altitude of 3,300 feet (1,000m), accompanied all the way by an impressive Alpine panorama, and an equally impressive gondola takes the visitor to **Männlichen**, while the Wengernalp railway goes to **Kleine Scheidegg** and **Wengernalp**. It is also from Grindelwald that one of the world's most famous rail journeys begins, first to Kleine Scheidegg and thence through the inside of the Eiger to the **Jungfraujoch**, from where you can enjoy an incomparable view of snow capped mountians. Particularly impressive are visits to the **upper Grindelwald glacier**, the **blue ice grotto**, and the **lower Grindelwald glacier**, with its romantic, narrow glacial gorge.

Tourist Office: Sportzentrum, CH-3818 Grindelwald (tel: (036) 531212)

◆◆◆ (summer)
◆◆◆ (winter)
GSTAAD

Although it has the reputation of being the resort of the 'jet set', this is only one side of Gstaad, and its range of hotels and amenities ensures that anyone can have an enjoyable stay here. One of Switzerland's most elegant resorts, it offers excellent facilities for both skier and non-skier, the surrounding 'white highland'

CENTRAL SWITZERLAND

region – including Saanen, Schönried and Rougemont – being superb. One pass covers the entire lift network, all local buses and trains between the resorts, plus entrance to Gstaad's heated indoor swimming pool.

Among this year-round resort's many other facilities are open air and indoor ice rinks for skating plus one open air and four indoor rinks for curling (the Jackson cup, the greatest curling prize in Europe is competed for at Gstaad); a three-mile (5km) toboggan run; sauna, massage, and children's pool; indoor tennis and squash courts; plenty of paths for walkers; horses for hire and an indoor riding hall.

Hotels

The five-star **Palace Hotel** is everything a hotel of this standing should be, with attentive staff, excellent standards and good facilities. Also recommended are the **Bellevue Grand**, set in a delightful garden, and the charming **Hotel Olden**. More modest accommodation is rather more difficult to find.

Entertainment

There is an exceptional choice, ranging from sophisticated night spots to *Stüblis* where you can relax with a drink in a cosy atmosphere. Of special note is **La Cave**, in the basement of the **Hotel Olden**, while the **Greengo** at the Palace features internationally known bands. The **Chesery**, despite its vast dimensions, is also enjoyable.

Tourist Office: Hauptstrasse, CH-3780 Gstaad (tel: (030) 47171)

◆◆◆ (summer)
◆◆ (winter)
INTERLAKEN ✓

Set between the sparkling waters of Lake Thun (Thuner See) and Lake Brienz, (Brienzer See), Interlaken enjoys a magnificent setting on the banks of the River Aare.

One of Switzerland's longest-established holiday resorts, Interlaken lies in the heart of the country, in the Bernese Oberland, at an altitude of 1,864 feet (568m) and offers a wide range of facilities and amenities for sport, entertainment and excursions in the surrounding area. The **Jungfraujoch** and its famous railway station – the highest in Europe – or the **Schilthorn**, with its famous mountaintop revolving restaurant are just two possible trips.

With a capacity of some 4,500 beds, ranging from the modest guest house to the top luxury class grand hotel, the resort is well provided to meet the tastes and pockets of most visitors.

The main promenade, the **'Höheweg'** (known as the 'Höhe'), is lined with flowers and fronted by a huge open meadow from where you can enjoy one of the most famous views in the world with unimpeded vistas of snow-dusted mountains. Along the Höheweg are many of Interlaken's hotels, a selection of restaurants, tea rooms and

The Kursaal Casino, standing in beautiful gardens, is Interlaken's social and cultural centre

fashionable shops, not to mention the Kursaal Casino. Interlaken has large open-air and indoor heated swimming pools, a covered artificial ice rink and covered tennis courts, while in summer the nearby lakes offer opportunities for sailing, windsurfing, fishing and waterskiing as well as several lakeside beaches. Mini-golf, golf – there is an 18-hole lakeside course – and riding are also available.

Skiing
Interlaken's strategic location as gateway to the Bernese Oberland makes it a popular choice with those who do not mind having no ski slope on their doorstep but who use the lakeside resort as a base to visit different ski regions during the day.

Hotels
Combining an atmosphere of elegance, comfort and style, the **Hotel Beau Rivage**, on the Höheweg, is set in its own grounds by the River Aare, a few minutes' walk from Interlaken's centre. In the mid-price bracket, the **Beau-Site** at Seestrasse 16, also surrounded by its own gardens, is recommended. On the northside of the town, the Hirschen is a comfortable guesthouse run by the same family for nine generations.

Entertainment

There are a number of nightspots, discos, bars and cosy *Stüblis*, while each week in the winter usually sees a lively folklore evening. There is a night-club with live music, dancing and entertainment at the **Victoria-Jungfrau Hotel**, Höheweg 41; a popular pub at the **Hotel Splendid**, Höheweg 33; and typical rustic-style *Stüblis* at the **Hirschen** and **Kreuz** hotels.

In July and August there are romantic cruises with dancing on Lake Thun and special open-air performances in Interlaken itself of Schiller's drama *Wilhelm Tell*.

Restaurants

La Terrace at the Vicroria-Jungfrau Hotel is the best in town. Also good is the **Hirschen**, and the **Lotus**, Interlaken's only chinese restaurant. Afternoon tea at the **Café Schuh** is a 'must'.

Excursions

Lovely small villages are within easy access of Interlaken by means of the vintage steamers which ply the bigger, but shallower, of Interlaken's lakes, the Lake of Thun (Thuner See), or by car or train along the shore. Among the most interesting are

Train near Wengen: part of the spectacular mountain railway system

Oberhofen, noted for its medieval castle; **Spiez**, on the south shore of the lake, with an impressive castle and a fascinating museum; and **Thun**, at the far end of the lake, which also boasts a romantic castle as well as a museum.

Top of most visitors' list is a trip on the **Jungfrau Railway**, providing spectacular mountain scenery and the experience of actually passing through the Eiger mountain on the way to Jungfraujoch, Europe's highest railway station at 11,333 feet (3,454m). From the terrace of the Jungfraujoch Plateau there are fine views of the Aletchgletscher, the longest glacier in the Alps.

Tourist Office: Höheweg 37, CH-3800 Interlaken (tel: (036) 222121)

◆◆◆ (summer)
◆◆ (winter)
LUZERN (LUCERNE) ✓

Luzern may lack the cosmopolitanism of Zürich, Geneva or Bern, but it is surely the most delightful of Switzerland's cities, small enough to be walked round easily and with an excellent selection of hotels, restaurants, shops and sightseeing possibilities coupled with a magnificent setting.

Standing in the foothills of the St Gotthard Pass, Luzern borders the lake of the same name, which winds deep into the Alpine ranges of central Switzerland. Here, the gentle waterscape contrasts with wild, majestic scenery and, not surprisingly, lake excursions are high on the list of visitors' priorities.

The Lake Luzern Navigation company provides large and comfortable steamers and a wide selection of half- or full-day excursions which can be combined with a trip to the top of a mountain. The company operates 18 boats, five of them paddle steamers, and there are boat departures every hour, with a restaurant on board some services.

Sightseeing

Seeing the sights of Luzern on foot is a joy. You can stroll alongside the River Reuss, sample the delightful atmosphere, and marvel at the **Kapellbrücke** (Chapel Bridge), built in 1333, and recently restored after a fire. With its numerous gable paintings and sturdy water tower, it is the city's unmistakable landmark. Near by are quaint alleys, and enchanting medieval buildings. In the city's arcades, on Tuesdays and Saturdays in particular, you can enjoy the hustle and bustle of the market crowd as you shop.

One of Switzerland's most popular museums is the **Verkehrshaus der Schweiz** (Swiss Transport Museum). Situated on the Luzern lakeside at Lidostrasse 5, the museum is reached from the centre of town by car, bus or ferryboat. The museum traces the history, development and importance of transport on land, water and in the air and is one of the largest and most comprehensive collections of its kind in Europe.

Open: daily.

CENTRAL SWITZERLAND

Hotels

The recently refurbished **Palace Hotel**, Haldenstrasse 10, dating from the end of the last century, is a delight, as are the 600 year old **Zum Rebstock** in the heart of the city at St Leodegarstrasse, and the **Grand Hotel National**, on the lakeshore at Haldenstrasse 4. In the moderate price bracket try the **Hotel Des Alpes** at Rathausquai 5.

Entertainment

Luzern boasts a wide range of sporting opportunities, from freshwater beaches to scenic golfing, with international horse-races, and rowing regattas on the Rotsee, traditional annual events.

By car it is only an hour to Engelberg, a superbly equipped winter sports area, while winter is also the season for Luzern's intriguing folk festival, *Fasnacht or Mardi Gras*.

Restaurants

Among the best in town are **Chez Marianne**, the **Old Swiss House**, beim Löwendenkmal, and the **Barbatti**, which is located in a 19th-century building.

Excursions

The proud rock pyramid of **Mount Pilatus** is one of the chief landmarks of Luzern. The summit can be reached in two different ways. From Kriens (12 minutes by bus from Luzern), the four-seater cabins of a cablecar glide over fertile meadows and green forests to Fräkmüntegg. From there an aerial cableway – a daring feat of engineering – swings along

the steep cliff carrying visitors up to the peak, both in summer and winter.

From the end of April to the beginning of November the world-famous electric Pilatus railway climbs the mountain from Alpnachstad to Pilatus-Kulm. With a maximum gradient of 48°, this is the steepest cogwheel railway in the world. The way to Alpnachstad is along the shores of Lake Luzern by steamer, the Brünig railway, or by car.

The circular tour from Luzern-Alpnachstad up to Pilatus-Kulm and down to Kriens-Luzern is unforgettable. Among the many delightful small towns and

villages easily accessible from Luzern are **Zug**, standing on the shores of lake Zug and set among orchards and gardens; **Gersau**, where laurels, chestnuts and fig trees grow in the mild climate; **Schwyz**, from which the country takes its name; **Hergiswil**, a pleasant, peaceful lakeside resort; and **Bürgenstock**, where numerous film stars and celebrities have homes.

Tourist Office: Frankenstrasse 1, CH-6002 Luzern (tel: (041) 517171)

Luzern's 14th-century Kapellbrücke with the even older Water Tower

◆◆◆ (summer)
◆◆ (winter)
MÜRREN
Set in a superb position on a mountain terrace facing the Jungfrau and the Eiger, Mürren has long been a popular choice with visitors, especially winter sports enthusiasts, even though the choice for skiing is not as great as in some of Switzerland's bigger resorts. It is traffic free, as no roads lead to the resort, the village being reached, instead, either by funicular from Lauterbrunnen or by the 4-stage Schilthorn cable car from Stechelberg.
It is a very picturesque, unspoilt village which, with its wooden chalets and narrow winding alleys, has great charm and character. The Schilthorn towers above the resort and at its 10,000-foot (3,048m) summit there is a superb revolving restaurant which was featured in the James Bond film *On Her Majesty's Secret Service*.
There are easy nursery slopes in the centre of the village, and beginners are taken up to Allmendhubel with its gentle slopes and a drag lift to make things easier. There are special classes for children from three years of age.
Other sports facilities include an excellent leisure centre with indoor pool, whirlpool, squash courts, gymnasium, ice rink and a library, and there are also indoor tennis courts, a sauna and solarium, as well as a network of paths for walking.
A kindergarten for children under three is available in the mornings, and for children from three to six from 09.30 to 16.30

hours except Saturday and
Sunday.

Hotels

The **Eiger** and the **Blumental**
both enjoy excellent reputations.
The **Hotel Alpina** is a family-run
guest house whose restaurant
enjoys an unrivalled view.

Tourist Office: Sportzentrum,
CH-3825 Mürren (tel: (036)
551616)

◆◆ (summer)
◆ (winter)
WEGGIS

This little resort with its flower-
decked promenades, lakeside
lido and mild, sunny climate, is
about 40 minutes by lake
steamer from Luzern.
A good spot for a relaxing break,
Weggis offers a variety of
excellent leisure facilities
including a heated indoor
swimming pool, outdoor tennis
courts, fishing, sailing and
windsurfing. Each morning in the
high season you can enjoy a
concert on the lakeside
bandstand or in one of the hotels.
There are numerous walks in the
hills behind Weggis and, there
are concerts and folklore
evenings throughout the
summer. The 'Rose Festival',
hosted each year by Weggis
and including music, dancing
and a fireworks display, takes
place the last weekend in June.

Hotels

Set in beautiful grounds which
provide flowers for the hotel and
fresh fruit and vegetables for the
kitchen, the **Park Hotel** enjoys a
quiet, lakeside location.

Tourist Office: CH-6353 Weggis
(tel: (041) 931155)

◆◆◆ (summer)
◆◆◆ (winter)
WENGEN

Wengen is a perfect place for
relaxing and unwinding –
there is very little to disturb the
peace, not even a road up from
the Lauterbrunnen valley.
Instead, everyone and
everything comes here by the
mountain railway which
continues on up to Kleine
Scheidegg and the Jungfraujoch
and which also links Wengen
with Grindelwald.
The resort's real advantage is
the direct access to the whole
Jungfrau region, by means of

either the mountain railway to Wengernalp or the cable car to the top of the Männlichen from where there is an enormous choice of runs.

In summer this friendly resort offers many walks around the village, along a network of paths which take you through mountain woods and flower-filled meadows with views of the Jungfrau Glacier and over the valley to the Schilthorn.

Hotels

The 5-star **Park Hotel Beausite** enjoys a peaceful location set back from the village centre with

The quiet little resort of Wengen is a gateway to the Jungfrau region

beautiful views of the Jungfrau range, and offers traditional Swiss hospitality in luxurious surroundings – including an indoor pool. The **Falken** is a superb old museum on the fringe of the village.

Entertainment

You will not find the sophistication or the choice of St Moritz or Davos here, but there is still plenty to do in the evenings. Both the **Pickel Bar** and the **Tanne Stübli** are popular, and usually packed;

and the **Arvenstube** offers a good atmosphere, often with an accordianist playing.

The **Silberhornstube** is another spot with a casual, relaxed atmosphere and live music. For a lively evening with music you could try **The Pub** nightspot, **Tiffany's Disco** or the **Paradiso Disco**. The **Carousel** has a live group and a more sophisticated atmosphere.

Tourist Office: CH-3823 Wengen (tel: (036) 551414)

◆◆◆ (summer)
◆◆ (winter)
WILDERSWIL

This picture-postcard village with its traditional old chalets decked in summer with pink and red pelargoniums, its green fields and meadows and beautiful panoramic views. The village is an ideal starting point for easy walks through the meadows and on the lower mountain slopes.

Not to be missed is a trip on the rack-and-pinion railway which leads up from Wilderswil to the

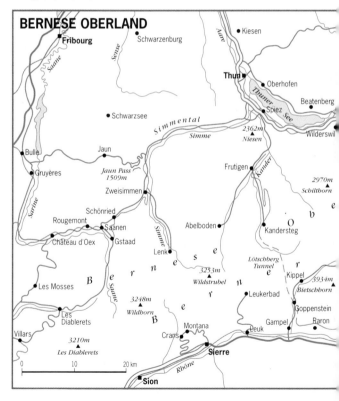

BERNESE OBERLAND

famous **Alpine Garden** at Schynige Platte.

Hotels

The **Hotel Schlössli** is a little chalet-style hotel set in an idyllic location on the edge of Wilderswil village. The **Victoria** is a better bet for families.

Tourist Office: Lehngasse, CH-3812 (tel: (036) 228455)

A popular excursion from Wilderswil is to the Schynige Platte, with its views and Alpine Garden

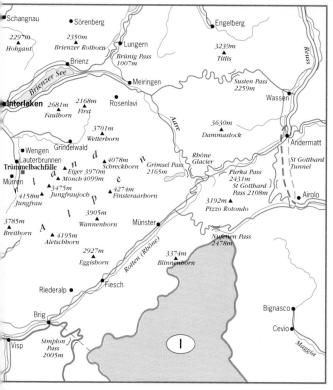

THE GRISONS (GRAUBUNDEN)

The largest of Switzerland's cantons, covering about a sixth of the country's land mass, the Grisons is also the only one where three languages – German, Italian and Romansch – are spoken. It comprises remote farms and villages and numerous popular holiday resorts such as glitzy St Moritz, Davos, Flims and Klosters. Capital of the Grisons is the ancient cathedral city of Chur.

◆◆ (summer)
◆◆◆ (winter)
AROSA

This long-established and popular resort is an attractive and lively village remotely set in superb scenery at the head of the spectacular Plessur Valley. A resort that combines much of the sophistication of St Moritz with the casual, relaxed atmosphere of many smaller Swiss resorts, Arosa has accommodation ranging from five-star de luxe hotels to small family *pensions*.

For winter sports enthusiasts, however, there are varied slopes and, although there are no very difficult runs for the really expert skier, there is plenty to satisfy the intermediate or good skier. All the ski areas are interconnecting and form a well-planned and efficient network with over 45 miles (72km) of downhill runs which are prepared and patrolled. *Langlauf* (cross-country skiing) is popular with visitors to Arosa, and there are nearly 20 miles (32km) of special pistes.

Other resort facilities include a toboggan run, two natural ice-skating rinks and two artificial rinks, tennis and squash facilities, horse-riding, bowling alleys and a casino, as well as paths for walking.

At the **Park Hotel** a kindergarten operates from 09.00 to 18.00 hours Monday to Friday, free of charge to hotel guests.

Hotels

The **Arosa Kulm Hotel** is located in a prime position in inner Arosa and offers a good range of facilities. The **Waldhotel-National** is situated in its own park amid pine woods, a few minutes' walk from the village. The old-fashioned **Betri**, opposite the museum, has plenty of character.

Entertainment

This ranges from the casual to the sophisticated. There is a casino with gaming room and a smart disco bar, plus the **'Nuts'** disco for the younger guests. Other Arosa nightspots include the **Rondo** with live music and a casual atmosphere; the **Taverna**, with Wurlitzer juke box; and the **Garda Bar** with show bands and folklore. The **Valsana** has an orchestra and the **Tschuggen** and **Kulm** both have smart nightspots. From time to time there are ice galas and ice hockey matches, while the horse-races on snow are one of the highlights of the season.

Restaurants

Try one of the two excellent restaurants in the Merkur, or the themed and candlelit Saumer

Winter view of Arosa, sheltered in its hollow, across the ski slopes

Stube where the staff wear 17th century costume. During après-ski the place to be seen is **Kaiser's** tearoom.

Excursion

The 20-minute cable car journey to the top of **Weisshorn** at 8,704 feet (2,653m) is rewarded by the magnificent panorama of the snowy ridges of the Grisons Alps.

Tourist Office: CH-7050 Arosa (tel: (081) 311621)

◆◆ (summer)
◆◆ (winter)

CHUR

Chur (pronounced 'Koor') is still a major junction and many never get beyond the railway station – which is a pity because there is much to see, and 'doing the sights' here is made simple by red and green footprints which lead you through the town's nooks and crannies right to the historic places. However, care should be taken in following the trails, as the markings are so unobtrusive that it is easy to lose your way. The red trail takes you first to the 15th-century Gothic **Rathus** (town hall), and eventually to the **Rhätisches Museum** (Rhaetic Museum), taking in various sights on the way.

The green path leads you to the Plessur, a tributary of the Rhein, and to the **Upper Gate**.

THE GRISONS

The **Bischöflicher Schloss** (Bishop's Palace) and the **Cathedral of Our Lady** are quickly reached by following the steps through the tower gate. The cathedral impresses with its sheer massiveness, while the cathedral, treasury bears witness to the centuries-old religious heritage of the city. Also of interest are:

The **Kunstmuseum** (Fine Arts Museum) in Postplatz, with important works by Swiss artists among others.

Open: daily during exhibitions, except Mondays.

A private **carriage collection** from the 19th century, in the Romantik Hotel Stern.

Open: daily.

Hotels

The **Romantik Hotel Stern**, Reichgasse 11, occupying a 17th-century building with rustic decor, is very good.

Restaurants

Excellent food can be enjoyed in the restaurant of the **Rebleuten Hotel**, and at **Zum Alten Zollhaus**, occupying part of the former customs house. Among the many prosperous and convivial inns, the **Drei Könige** is noteworthy.

Excursions

Chur is an excursion hub. The narrow-gauge Rhaetian Railway is a fun way of visiting **Arosa** and the **Engadine**, **Davos** or **Disentis** with its Benedictine monastery in baroque style. The yellow coaches of the Swiss Alpine Post will carry you to **Lenzerheide**, **St Moritz**, or **Flims**; or over the **Splügen Pass** and

San Bernardino to the **Ticino**.

Tourist Office: Ottostrasse 6, CH-7000 Chur (tel: (081) 221818)

◆◆ (summer)
◆◆◆ (winter)
DAVOS

Davos is one of Switzerland's premier ski resorts, providing some of the best winter skiing in the world, with a fine lift system, reliable snow conditions and a host of après-ski facilities. Located in a peaceful Alpine valley, it is divided into two parts – **Platz** and **Dorf** – (but without any clear distinction between the two) and is a lively, if architecturally undistinguished place with a number of charming restaurants, cafés and stylish boutiques. It has a long history as a health resort, and was famously patronised by Robert Louis Stevenson and Sir Arthur Conan-Doyle amongst other 19th century notables. With 12,000 inhabitants, Davos is even larger than St Moritz, offering 17 hotels with 6,500 beds during the winter season, and in summer 4,600 beds in hotels and boarding houses. About 10,000 beds in rented apartments and private rooms are available all year.

Winter Sports

Davos is the largest ski resort of the Grisons. The ski slopes that attract the crowds are on the sides of the Strela chain of mountains, dominated by the Weissfluhjoch. The **Parsenn funicular railway** gives access to the most remarkable snow fields in the country, taking skiers from Davos up to Weissfluhjoch, nearly 9,000 feet (2,750m) high,

and the top of the Parsenn run.
From there they can ski down
3,500 feet (1,000m) to the town,
or, take a northwesterly route to
reach the neighbouring resort of
Klosters (see page 53).
Another funicular, combined
with a gondola, goes to **Strela**
and by a junction line to the
Parsenn area. On the left side of
the Davos Valley is the well-
equipped **Brämabüel –
Jakobshorn** ski area, reached
by cable car and skilifts. **Pischa**,
a ski station situated in the Flüela
Valley and reached by bus from
Davos-Dorf, offers ski runs
situated on the south and sunny
face of the mountain.
In **Glaris**, just to the south of
Davos, is a chairlift to the
Rinerhorn (7,500 feet/2,200m).
Over 50 miles (80km) of cross-
country ski tracks are well
prepared. Ski instructors of the
Swiss Ski School teach children
and adults in downhill skiing and
cross-country skiing, and
special weekly arrangements
known as White Weeks,
combining skiing and/or cross-
country skiing are popular in
December, January and April.

Summer Facilities
In summer Davos is equally
delightful. It has 200 miles
(320km) of well-kept walks and
paths through town, mountains
and forest; climbing and
mountaineering weeks are
organised; and the resort offers
sailing, windsurfing, swimming

*Skating sometimes provides an
alternative to skiing at Davos*

in the Lake of Davos or the open air and indoor swimming pools, trout fishing in either the lake or the Landwasser River and its tributaries, golf on an 18-hole course, horseback riding and tennis.

A children's playground is set in the middle of town, and there are numerous picnic places in the surroundings.

Walks

A walk (one hour there and back) can be made along the **Hohe Promenade**, a perfectly planned walk, level, sometimes under trees, and kept clear of snow in winter. It may be reached from Davos-Dorf from near the Parsenn funicular station or from Davos-Platz by a steep path leading up to the Catholic church.

The countryside around Davos provides endless walking possibilities through meadows, past farms and up into the mountains with magnificent views all around. For a more leisurely ascent to the peak, a variety of cable cars and funiculars is available from mid-June, taking visitors up to **Jakobshorn** at 8,500 feet (2,600m) or the **Parsenn** at 9,200 feet (2,800m), while the five-minute funicular ride up to **Schatzalp** should not be missed. You can visit the **Alpine Flower Garden** and return on foot through the pine woods with squirrels at practically every bend.

Hotels and Restaurants

The **Steigenberger Belvedere** is a 'grand' hotel in the true sense of the word, and enjoys a superb situation with views over

the valley towards the Jakobshorn. Also recommended is the **Central Sporthotel**, noted for its attentive service. The **Hotel Edelweiss** offers simple, family accommodation in Davos-Dorf. Notable restaurants include the **Bundnerstübli** and the reasonably priced **Red Lion Bar**. For an excellent fondue try the **Gentiana** – and for delicious pastries and hot chocolate either the **Café Fah** or **Schneider's**.

Entertainment

Popular spots are the **Postli Club** with top groups and showbands and the **Montana**, with live music and dancing.The younger crowd favour the **Café Carlos**, the **Express Bar** and the **Cabana**, while for a real Swiss atmosphere with folklore there is the popular **Cava Grischa**.

Tourist Office: CH-7270 Daros Platz (tel: (081) 452121).

◆◆ (summer)
◆◆ (winter)
FLIMS

Flims ranks among the best-known tourist resorts of the Grisons. It is set on a terrace above the Rhein gorge amid spectacular scenery, and although considerably extended in recent years it is still esentially a village resort – in fact two villages: **Flims-Dorf**, the traditional residential section and **Flims-Waldhaus**, whose hotels are scattered through a forest of conifers. The nearby village of **Laax** also shares the same ski area, known as 'the white arena'.

Among Flims's many facilities are cross-country ski trails

Corvatsch. Here snow is virtually guaranteed (the upper slopes are also used for summer skiing) and conditions are ideal for late-season skiing.

In summer, the chief appeal of St Moritz lies in the wide range of sports facilities available, such as summer skiing, sailing, windsurfing, tennis, horseback riding, golf on the highest and oldest 18-hole golf course in continental Europe, ice-skating and other activities, all found within a 20 minutes' driving radius.

The stunning Upper Engadine landscape with its 25 mountain lakes, four of which are ideal for sailing and windsurfing, all add to the attractions, as do the health spa, the numerous cultural programmes, and the **Swiss National Park**, within an hour's drive.

Pontresina

Pontresina is a small village resort with buildings in the typical Engadine painted style, which lies in a sheltered valley at 6,000 feet (1,800m) just ten minutes by train from St Moritz and sharing the same ski area. It is much less sophisticated than St Moritz, but is a charming resort nevertheless – and much cheaper and friendlier than its neighbour!

Hotels and Restaurants

The well-heeled visitor to St Moritz is spoiled for choice of excellent hotels, the **Carlton**, **Palace** and **Suvretta House** being among the best. The moderately priced **Soldanella** is also recommended. Of the numerous excellent restaurants,

St Moritz is Switzerland's most chic resort, especially in winter

the most fashionable include **Chesa Veglia**; the **Rôtisserie des Chevaliers** at the **Kulm Hotel**; and the **Grotto**. In Pontresina, **Pension Edelweiss** is a charming chalet-style hotel offering inexpensive accommodation.

Entertainment

The entertainment available in St Moritz is wide ranging, with horse-racing on the frozen lake in January and February, a casino, fashion shows, night-clubs, discos, cafés, cinemas, concerts, galas and competitions.

Tourist Office: via Maistra 12, CH-7500 St Moritz (tel: (082) 33147)

SOUTHERN SWITZERLAND

This region is the location of the Italian-speaking Ticino region, with its delightful lakeland areas and resorts such as Locarno and Lugano; and it is also home of the area known as the Valais (Wallis in German), with the mighty River Rhône at its core, bounded by some of the highest peaks in the Alps. It is here that one finds some of Switzerland's most attractive sports resorts, including Crans/Montana, Saas-Fee, Verbier and Zermatt.

◆◆◆ (summer)
◆◆ (winter)

ASCONA

Situated in a picturesque bay on Lake Maggiore, close to Locarno, Ascona owes its fame to artists. Exhibitions in the cultural Centre and the Museum for Modern Art, countless galleries and antique shops, readings and lectures, bear witness to its active cultural life. Giovanni Serodine, arguably the most talented painter from the Ticino, lived here in the 17th century. Three of his paintings are hung in the church of **Santi Pietro e Paolo**.

The **Collegio Pontificio Papio** was endowed in the 16th century by Bartolemeo Papio, a native of Ascona. The former sanctuary today serves as a secondary school. Its splendid renaissance court is decorated with the coats of arms of sponsors and protectors over a period of five centuries. **Santa Maria della Misericordia**, a church attached to the college, contains valuable frescos.

Palm trees nod to snowy peaks across Lake Maggiore at Ascona

Ascona caters for its guests in 50 hotels with a total of 3,100 beds, and a further 5,400 in holiday apartments and private accommodation. There is an underground car park in the centre and further parking facilities by the lake and on entering the town.

Hotels and Restaurants

Amongst a wide choice of luxury hotels, the 5 star **Giardino** on the fringe of town stands out. At the budget end, the **Riposo** has a rooftop swimming pool. The **Ristorante Borromeo** offers splendid food in a rustic atmosphere.

Sports and Entertainment

Ascona has a wide range of sports and entertainment to offer its guests: riding, golf (18 holes), tennis, squash, swimming, windsurfing, sailing, waterskiing, as well as an ice rink for skating and curling. Attractive, well-maintained paths for walking and hiking open up the area round the town, and there is also a fitness track and a cycling path from Ascona to Bellinzona, which follows the lake for some distance but also passes through the fields in the Magadino plain. Drawing courses are offered regularly both in hotels and in the open air, and courses in bookbinding are also available.

Culture

For more than 40 years the annual international music festival held from August to October has presented classical concerts with world-famous conductors, orchestras and soloists, while another major attraction is the New Orleans Jazz Festival lasting

10 days in June and July, when Ascona's picturesque squares and alleys take on a particularly lively and colourful atmosphere.

Excursions

To get a feel of the countryside, you should visit **Ronco**, a picturesque village set a short distance to the west, high above Lake Maggiore. The isolated valleys above Ronco are worth exploring. The most rustic, **Val Verzasca**, can be reached by car or postbus.

Tourist Office: Casa Serodine, viale Papio, CH-6612 Ascona (tel: (093) 350090)

◆◆ (summer)
◆ (winter)
BELLINZONA

The capital city of the Ticino is an important industrial centre and rail transport hub, being located half-way between the fruitful Lombard Plain of Italy and the rugged Swiss Alps. The town has much to interest and fascinate, not least three castles and the ancient city walls. The oldest and largest of the castles, the **Castello Grande**, (or **Castle of Uri**) first mentioned in documents of the 6th century, has superb defences. The immense courtyard, which can be visited, was used in times of crisis as a refuge by the entire population. Steep walkways lead from the old city to the castle's heights. The ancient walls have been well preserved, and still link Castello Grande and its counterpart **Castello di Montebello** (or **Schwyz**). This castle originated in the late 13th or early 14th century and was subsequently

destroyed and restored on numerous occasions. Its main tower and *palazzetto* encompass a small museum featuring both history and archaeology.
Open: daily except Mondays.
High above the city is the **Castello di Sasso Corbaro**, (or **Unterwalden**), built in 1479 in just six months. Several rooms in its tower are dedicated to a collection of folk art and folklore.
Open: daily except Monday, April–October.
Bellinzona's three forts are still referred to as the castles of **Uri**, **Schwyz** and **Unterwald**.
The old city down below has elegant façades of patrician houses, ornamental iron balconies and gateways, rococo portals and fine inn signs.

Hotels
The **Hotel Unione**, via GL-Guisan, is a simple hotel, set in delightful gardens. The **San Giovanni** provides good, plain accommodation.

Excursions
A trip by car or postbus leads into the lonely yet enchanting **Valle Morobbia** and its chestnut forests. The sunny terrace of **Mornera**, a rewarding vantage point for the areas, can be reached by aerial cableway. Not to be missed is the '**Climbing Garden**' at **Molinazzo**.

Tourist Office: Palazzo Civico, via Camminata (tel: (092) 252131)

◆◆ (summer)
◆◆◆ (winter)
CRANS-MONTANA
At the heart of the Alps a large plateau covered with pine forests and scattered lakes faces the highest mountains of Europe,

Few golf courses can boast such a splendid view as this one at Crans-Montana

from the Matterhorn to Mont Blanc. Set on this sunny plateau at 5,000 feet (1,500km), with a spectacular view of the Rhône valley, are the adjoining villages of Crans (Crans-sur-Sierre to give it its full name) and Montana. In summer, there are many delightful walks through beautiful mountain scenery, following the lakeside or crossing the mountainside through forests. Cable cars take you up to 10,000 feet (3,000m) for even more spectacular scenery and views across the Valais from the many belvederes. For instance, a cable car from Crans makes a magnificent ascent over the Rhône valley to **Bella Lui** at 8,340 feet (2,543m).

The resort offers summer visitors any number of leisure activities. You can enjoy the facilities of the new sports and leisure complex, sunbathe and swim on the shores of **Lake Moubra**, play golf on what must be one of the most panoramic golf courses in the Alps, try your skills at ice-skating on the artificial ice rink, go horse-riding, or play tennis. As a winter resort, Crans-Montana has gained considerably in popularity in recent years, and is now one of the leading resorts in Switzerland, with an excellent record for snow, plenty of ski runs to appeal to the beginner and the intermediate skier, and nearly 100 miles (160km) of prepared pistes.

Hotels

The **Hotel Crans Ambassador** enjoys an enviable position just above Montana with lovely panoramic views over Lake Grenon and towards the

mountains. It is rivalled for views by the more moderately priced **Mont-Blanc**.

Entertainment

In Crans, The **George and Dragon** pub is a lively and popular bar; **Valentino's** is smarter and more sophisticated; and the **Sporting Club** is a select nightspot with live music and dancing and a gaming room. Montana has **Le Mazot** with an orchestra, dancing and cabaret, and the even classier **Number One**.

Excursions

Interesting excursions are possible to the traffic-free resort of **Zermatt** or the magnificent **Val d'Anniviers** and the picturesque villages of **Zinal** and **Grimentz**.

Tourist Office: CH-3963 Crans-sur-Sierre (tel: (027) 412132); avenue de la Gare, CH-3962 Montana (tel: (027) 413041)

◆◆◆ (summer)
◆ (winter)
LOCARNO

On the shores of Lake Maggiore, Locarno is a combination of resort and business centre. It has its old town where patrician houses look simple on the outside yet are magnificent inside, with old and cosy streets so narrow one can touch the walls of the opposite houses by stretching one's arms. And there is modern Locarno with department stores, wide avenues and all the up-to-date facilities of a tourist resort. The town boasts many historical sights. **Madonna del Sasso**, the pilgrimage church, is Locarno's

SOUTHERN SWITZERLAND

The pilgrimage church of Madonna del Sasso, on a crag above Locarno

emblem, reached by funicular from Contrada Cappuccini. The **Castello Visconti** (also known as **Rusca**) once served as a fortress and was the largest of its kind in Ticino; today it houses the **archaeological museum** with its rich collection of local prehistoric and Roman finds. *Open*: daily (except Mondays) from April to October.

The various, churches in Locarno are well worth a visit: **Sant' Antonio**, with its magnificent marble altars; **Chiesa Nuova**, with its stucco ceiling and relics; **San Vittore**, one of the major Romanesque sacred buildings in the Ticino; and **Santa Maria in Selva**, which has fine 15th-century frescos.

Culture

Locarno's International Film Festival held every August is one of the main cultural events in the Ticino, and the music festival held from May to July has become a popular meeting place for music-lovers.

Facilities

Locarno has been busy adding to its visitor facilities, increasing the number of open air swimming pools and improving its tennis courts located along the lake. Watersports are also available, and there is an 18-hole golf course only five minutes away by car. For the more adventurous there are courses in parachuting and para-gliding. Along the lakeshore promenade, subtropical trees, shrubs and flowers have been planted and are lovingly cared for.

Hotels and Restaurants
The **Palma au Lac** is Locarno's only five-star hotel, and it is a lovely place with a deservedly high reputation. Also recommended are the first-class **Reber au Lac** and **Grand Hotel**, and among the moderately priced establishments the **Beau Rivage**, many of whose rooms face the lake, and which has an *al fresco* restaurant in summer. Of the many good restaurants the **Panorama at the Dellaville Hotel**, **Centenario** and **Coq d'Or** are among the best – the **Citadella**, located in a centuries-old house in the old part of town, has a particularly good atmosphere.

Excursions
Locarno is ideally placed as an excursion centre for the magnificent **Ticino Valleys** stretching north to the **Leopontine Alps**. The **Valle Maggia**, and its tributary **Val Barona**, are amongst the most beautiful.
The town is also the main embarkation point for steamship trips on **Lake Maggiore** most unforgettably to the spellbinding subtropical paradise of the **Isles of Brissago**.

Tourist Office: Largo Zorzi CH-6601 Locarno (tel: (093) 310333)

◆◆◆ (summer)
◆ (winter)
LUGANO
Set between Monte Brè and Monte San Salvatore, Lake Lugano shimmers with light and colour, offering the visitor a sunny climate and a warm, lively atmosphere.
Lugano has preserved its fascinating traffic-free historic centre and is host to two of the most famous churches in Ticino: **San Lorenzo** and **St Mary of the Angels**.
Gardens and promenades fringe the lakeside from **Paradiso** towards **Castagnola**, from where a footpath continues to **Gandria**, one of the Ticino's most picturesque villages, which can also be reached by lake steamer.
The resort has two principal lidos for sunbathing and swimming, and waterskiing, windsurfing and sailing are also available. The less energetic may prefer to enjoy the scenery from one of the steamers which call regularly, or relax in one of the many pavement cafés and enjoy a cool drink while listening to one of the concerts which are frequently held in the piazza della Riformo or the lakeside gardens.

Hotels and Restaurants
The two most imposing hotels, both overlooking the lake, are the **Grand Hotel Eden** and the **Splendide Royale**. The most voguish is the elegant **Villa Principe Leopoldo**. Also recommended is the moderately priced **Hotel Ticino**, piazza Cioccara 1, set in a centuries-old house and refurbished in Città-Vecchia period style. One of the best restaurants in town is **Al Portone** in viole Casserate. Also excellent are **Bianchi** in via Pessina, and the locals' favourite – **Monte Cener** in via Nassa.

Entertainment

In the evenings, visitors have the choice between local bars, restaurants or sophisticated nightspots. Alternatively, a quiet stroll along the waterfront or an evening cruise with music may be more appealing.

The concert season runs from April to June followed by the lake festival at the end of July. The **Vintage Parade**, held on the first Sunday in October, is an event when the whole town comes together to have a good time.

Excursions

Just south of Lugano, near the valley of Morcote, **Swissminiatur** (Switzerland in Miniature) presents scale models of Swiss landmarks, including working models of trains and cable cars. *Open*: daily from mid-March to October.

Tourist Office: riva Albertolli 5, CH-6901 Lugano (tel: (091) 214664)

Lugano, with its flowers and mild climate, has an Italian aspect

◆◆◆ (summer)
◆◆ (winter)

THE GOMS VALLEY

Also known as the Conches Valley, or Upper Rhône Valley, this lateral 30 mile (48km) trench climbs west to east from the old trading centre of Brig to the high-lying glacier town of Gletsch. Scenery of increasing grandeur unfolds at every stage of this upward climb, and each new village appears to surpass its lower neighbour in charm and character. At Morel, five miles (7.5km) east of Brig, a cable-car ascends to the small but beautifully sited resort of Riederalp lying at a height of nearly 7,500 feet (2230 metres). A short distance from Morel is another lift to the summit of Moosfluh which provides a splendid view of the lower reaches of the Aletsch Glacier, the largest in Switzerland which starts its 17 mile (27km) descent from the south side of the Jungfrau massif. Rivalling Riederalp for location is the similarly sited mountain resort of Bettmeralp further east. Just before Fiesch, further along the valley, there is a road leading south of the charming old village of Ernen – well worth a detour. From Ernen a winding road climbs up the pastoral Binn valley to the remote and beautiful hamlets of Binn and Im Feld. From Fiesch itself there is another cable-car climbing in two stages to the Eggishorn which at an altitude of nearly 10,000 feet (3,000 metres) affords one of the finest views in the Valais. The Aletsch glacier sweeps down to the west, and to the east the Fiesch glacier appears poised to roll down onto the small hamlets beneath it. The next village of significance is Bellwald, reached either by narrow road or cable way two miles (3km) from Fiesch. An attractive huddle of typical larchwood chalets, it is surrounded to the north by a number of tiny hamlets each distinguished by ancient Alpine chapels. The view south from Bellwald is worth the diversion. The village of Niederwald, notable for its picturesque collection of traditional timber houses has earned modest fame as the birthplace of Cesar Ritz – the renowned hotelier whose name is now synonymous with luxurious surroundings. Reckingen, straddling the road ahead is notable for its handsome 18th-century baroque church complete with macabre glass-encased robed skeletons. The principal community of the Goms, Munster, lies beyond after which the valley becomes wilder and more mountainous. After the little village of Oberwald, the valley twists tortuously past the Rhône Falls until the canton border town of Gletsch with its electrifying view of the famous Rhône Glacier above.

Hotels

The main accommodation centres of the valley are at Riederalp and Bettmeralp. Recommended hotels in the former include the 4 star **Art Furrer** and the more modestly priced **Bergdohl**. A good value place in Bettmeralp is the **Alpfrieden**.

Tourist Office: CH-3981 Riederalp (tel: (028) 27 13 65)
Tourist Office: CH-3992 Bettmeralp (tel: (028) 27 12 91)

◆◆ (summer)
◆◆◆ (winter)
SAAS-FEE
The charming village of Saas-Fee in the Canton of Valais lies among magnificent mountains and glaciers in the heart of the highest Swiss Alps. No cars are allowed in the village itself, but transport is provided by horse-drawn sleigh or small electrically powered vehicles operated by the local taxi service as well as many hotels. One of the services offered by the Tourist Office, located near the bus station at the entrance to the village, is an electronic system which allows visitors to notify the hotel of their arrival; a hotel porter will then arrive with an electric car to transport the guests and their luggage.

The village of Saas-Fee has retained its Alpine flavour. Weather-beaten chalets and clusters of ancient barns are protected by the community, but some have been modernised to offer comfortable accommodation and shops. The 'Pearl of the Alps' as Saas-Fee is known, is surrounded by 13 lofty mountains. The Dom, 14,912 feet (4,545m) is the highest mountain completely within Swiss territory.

For winter skiers, it is one of the best resorts in Switzerland. The learner will find gentle slopes at the base of the mountain, while the enthusiast will delight in the black and red runs over the glaciers which run from three sides down into the valley. The 'Metro Alpin' (installed in 1984) is the world's highest

SOUTHERN SWITZERLAND

Restaurant overlooking Saas-Fee

underground funicular, running from Felskinn to Mittelallin. It takes skiers up to 11,500 feet (3,500m) where, of course, snow is always guaranteed. Summer mountaineering continues to be of prime importance, and the resort employs 40 guides in its mountaineering school. Programmes offered vary from easy tours to challenging climbs to the highest peaks. There are also ski-touring weeks in the spring and hiking weeks in the autumn.

Other facilities include tennis courts, a tennis school, public swimming pool with children's pool and sauna, miniature golf, horse-riding and bowling. Children aged three to six can be cared for in a kindergarten located in the village and supervised by a nurse.

Hotels and Restaurants

Saas-Fee has close to 7,500 beds in its 45 hotels and 1,300 chalets and apartments offering good standards of cleanliness, comfort and hospitality. Among the best are the **Grand Hotel** and the **Hotel Beau-Site**. Over 60 restaurants feature varied menus and friendly service, that at the **Waldhotel Fletschhorn** being outstanding.

Entertainment

The **Sans-Souci** at the **Grand Hotel** has a live group and a good atmosphere, while the **Yeti-Bar** with its rustic décor is also a popular dancing spot. The **Sissy**, **Nesti's**, and the **Go-Inn** are similarly energetic venues.

Excursions

Daily excursions are operated to various resorts such as **Zermatt** and **Chamonix**, while on the Felskinn visitors can see an **ice grotto** through an ice tunnel extending 200 feet (60m).

Tourist Office: CH-3906 Saas-Fee (tel: (028) 571457)

◆◆ (summer)
◆ (winter)

SION

The impression gained on approaching Sion is one of grandeur, the castle ruins of Tourbillon and its twin fortress-church Valère bestowing a sense of durability on the capital of the Valais, and emphasising its strong natural defensive position.

Signs of the Past

In 1961, at the edge of the River Sitter's erosion cone, in the 'Petit Chasseur', archaeologists discovered the earliest known evidence of Sion's settlement:

Sion with its twin fortified crags

one of the most important Neolithic (3000–1500BC) sites to be unearthed in Alpine regions. In the schoolyard of the Secondary School for Girls, several Stone Age monuments have been recovered, including dolmens, graves and monoliths.

Old Sion
The orange-coloured **Town Hall** is a magnificent building of the 17th century, with a domed tower, rich woodcarvings and wrought-iron embellishments. The latter are even more delicately executed on the

houses of the nobility that extend along Grand Pont and through its sidestreets. Hemmed in by the rue de Conthey and the rue de Lausanne is the most elegant building in the Valais, the **Maison Supersaxo**, built during the Renaissance but late Gothic in appearance.
Leaving the centre of the city along the Grand Pont, the visitor should roam through the old sector this side of the Sitter.

Museums
Approaching Valère along the Schlossgasse, the visitor passes the **Majorie** (formerly housing

episcopal officials), now the **Museum of Fine Arts**, and the **Archaeological Museum**, The fossil imprints of ancient Saurians found in the vicinity of Emosson are here.
Open: Tuesday to Sunday.
Valère houses the **Musée Cantonal d'Histoire et d'Ethnologie** (Museum of History and Ethnology). Its 40 rooms offer a glimpse into history and prehistoric times, while what is said to be the oldest playable organ in the world (1390) annually resounds during the International Festival of Old Organs.
Open: Tuesday to Sunday in summer.

Hotels and Restaurants
Recommended hotels include the **Hôtel du Rhône**, 10 rue du Scex and the **Hôtel Touring**, 6 avenue de la Gare. Among the best places to eat are the **Enclos de Valère** and the adjacent **Caves de Tous-Vent**.

Excursion
A spectacular sight is the **Lac Souterrain** (Underground Lake of St-Léonard), a little way out of Sion on the road to Brig.

Tourist Office: place de la Planta, Sion (tel: (027) 228586)

◆◆ (summer)
◆◆◆ (winter)
VERBIER
Verbier, dominated by the 9,800-foot (3,000m) high Mont Gelé, is an exceptionally well-equipped resort. Haphazard building and planning do not make it attractive, but nevertheless it offers superb skiing, making it one of the country's most popular winter sports resorts, especially with the younger crowd and the international community based in Genève.
There is a vast network of lifts,

Curling is one of the many sports to be enjoyed at Verbier in winter

cable cars and ski runs, with slopes for every kind of skier, from novice to professional, together with a good range of facilities for other sports and recreations.

Mont Gelé is reached by three cable cars; from Verbier take the cable car to Les Ruinettes, then change Attelas I and again for Attelas II. From the cross which indicates you are at the rocky summit of Mont Gelé, there are marvellous views of the Mont Blanc and Grand Combin massifs.

Hotels
There are many well-appointed hotels in the resort, the **Grand-Combin et Golf** and the **Rosalp** being particularly noteworthy.

Restaurants and Entertainment
The restaurant **Gastronomique Pierroz** at the **Rosalp** is highly recommended, while the **Café La Grange** and **L'Ecurie** serve Valaisannes specialities in a charming rustic setting.

For après-ski life The **Farm Club** is the most voguish venue in town.

Tourist Office: CH-1936 Verbier (tel: (026) 316222)

◆◆◆ (summer)
◆◆◆ (winter)
ZERMATT
Surrounded by some of Europe's highest mountains – the Dom, Matterhorn and Monte Rosa – and their great glaciers, Zermatt is one of the world's premier winter ski resorts, with near perfect skiing at an altitude which makes the snow conditions more reliable than at most other winter resorts.

There is no motor traffic, and the centre is beautifully maintained in traditional style, although cowsheds have given way to Rolex and Gucci shops and five-star hotels. It also boasts its own art gallery, the **Galerie Matterhorn**, and a museum.

The **Alpine Museum** contains relics of the first conquests of the Matterhorn together with a scale model of the mountain. There is also a reconstruction of 'old' Zermatt with traditional mountain-dwellers' homes.
Open: daily June to mid-October and mid-December to April.

Walks
Most guests visiting Zermatt in the summer come to view the Matterhorn, to walk on the mountain slopes surrounding this majestic mountain and to see the wealth of wild flowers found on the high Alpine pastures. There are short walks such as the half-hour stroll to the **Gorner** gorge with its waterfalls.

For a half-day walk you can take the **Gornergrat** rack railway, one of Europe's highest cogwheel railways, up to the Riffelberg, from where there is an excellent view of the Matterhorn and its glistening glaciers, and then walk down to Zermatt via Ritti and Winkelmatten.

Skiing
In winter Zermatt is a skier's paradise, with an excellent ski area for all grades, extensive uphill transport, ample mountain restaurants, and over 100 miles (160km) of prepared pistes.

The unmistakable outline of the Matterhorn backs the Gornergrat Railway at over 10,200 feet (3,100m)

Even the morning rush hour for the cable car has been alleviated by a new electric ski-bus service.

The new cable car takes you up to the **Klein Matterhorn** (Little Matterhorn), the highest ski station in Europe, with spectacular views over the mountain range, and a good, easy downhill run on the glaciers. There are also black runs for the 'aces', gentle slopes for beginners and off-piste skiing for the experienced deep-snow skiers, plus the latest artificial snow machines.

For those who prefer to take it more leisurely, there are plenty of aerial cable cars as well as the mountain train and the underground railway up to **Sunegga**.

Hotels and Restaurants
There are 106 hotels and guest houses accommodating 18,000 guests in Zermatt. Recommended are the **Hotel Monte Rosa**, one of the oldest in town and formerly patronised by Edward Whymper – the first man to climb the Matterhorn, and enjoying panoramic views, and the luxury **Hotel Mont Cervin**, in Bahnhofstrasse, a traditional-style hotel situated in the heart of the village, with a wide range of facilities, including an indoor swimming pool, sauna, solarium and kindergarten. The **Romantik Hotel Julen** is a more modest traditional-style hotel.
Of the many restaurants, the **Alex Grill at the Alex Hotel** is highly recommended, while for pastries and coffee, the **Hörnli** in Bahnhofstrasse is particularly good.

Entertainment
The **Matterhorn Stube** is a popular meeting place, and the lively nightspot at the **Hotel Pollux** has both disco and live music. Other popular discos are **Le Village** and the **Broken Ski Bar**, and for a little jazz try the **Pink Elephant**. **Elsies Bar** on Kirchplatz, is the most popular après-ski venue.

Tourist Office: Bahnhofplatz, CH-3920 Zermatt (tel: (028) 661181)

WESTERN SWITZERLAND

The western part of the country contains much to interest the visitor, including Lac Léman, otherwise known as the Lake of Geneva, which has long attracted poets, artists and composers; year-round holiday resorts such as cosmopolitan Montreux and Lausanne; and the sparsely-settled region known as the Jura, where watchmaking has been a cottage industry for centuries.

◆◆ (summer)
◆◆◆ (winter)
CHATEAU D'OEX

Lying midway between the Bernese Oberland and Lac Léman, Château d'Oex (pronounced 'day') is a traditional mountain village with chalet-style houses. It is fast becoming one of Switzerland's premier winter sports resorts. From **La Braye**, at 5,300 feet (1,615m), there are easy and medium ski runs with four drag lifts and runs of all degrees of difficulty back down to **Pra Perron**, reached from the resort by cable car. From La Braye there is also a long run down to the hamlet of **Gerignoz**, from where a chairlift will take you up to the ski area again or a free ski-bus service will bring you back to Château d'Oex.

In both winter and summer there are numerous walking trails through pine forests and meadows. A visit to the Nature Reserve of **La Pierreuse** to see the chamois is particularly popular, while the most spectacular cable car ride is that from **Diablerets** village – accessible by train and postbus

– to a glacier with superb views. Younger visitors are also attracted by white river rafting on the **River Sarine** – available from May to mid-August – and canoeing, while other popular sporting pastimes include fishing for trout in the Sarine or nearby lakes such as **Rossinière** and **L'Hongrin**.

Sports facilities in the resort itself include tennis, riding, mini-golf, cycling, rock-climbing and hot-air ballooning, and there is also a sports centre offering a multipurpose sports hall, fitness room, sauna and solarium. Although tourism is the mainstay of this valley, agriculture and craftsmanship also play an important role, reflected in the **Musée du Vieux Pays d'Enhaut** (Enhaut Traditional Museum), whose exhibits include a fine collection of engravings, paper silhouettes and stained glass windows.

Open: daily (except Mondays and Wednesdays and closed for most of October).

Also part of the museum, but located at the end of town, is the **Etambeau Chalet** (18th-century), which houses exhibitions of regional architecture.

Open: daily except Saturdays closed Sunday mornings.

Hotels

The **Bon-Accueil**, dating from 1756, has style; also popular is the **Beau-Séjour**.

Entertainment

The **Green Fizz** disco-piano bar is one of the most popular spots for dancing, while **La Ranch** and the **Rougemont** also offer lively discos. The **Keller Bar at the Bon-Accueil** has a great ambience. In addition, there are open-air musical concerts by visiting bands and choirs, several cafés where one can relax over a glass of wine – or you could take the cable car to a mountain farm for a Swiss evening.

Tourist Office: La Place, CH-1837 Château-d'Oex (tel: (029) 47788)

◆◆ (summer)
◆ (winter)
FRIBOURG

Fribourg does not reveal all its delights at first glance. One must get to know the town and its soul if one is to discover its true riches. Approaching it from the east, the visitor is greeted by a

Fribourg, clustered around its river, is an architectural treasure-trove

surprise as he comes round a bend in the road, for situated on a steep bluff traced by the deep and winding course of the River Sarine ('Saane' in German), the heart of the old town unfolds in all its medieval splendour.

Magnificently preserved and restored at great expense, period houses cluster about the **Cathédral Saint-Nicholas**, whose Gothic architecture contributes to the perpendicular effect of the location.

Fribourg is modest in terms of inhabitants (about 40,000), yet is impressive in terms of its protected historical buildings, its treasures of medieval religious art, its cosmopolitan population, and its importance as a centre of contemporary Christian thought.

A bilingual Catholic university, founded in 1899 and the only one in Switzerland, a renowned

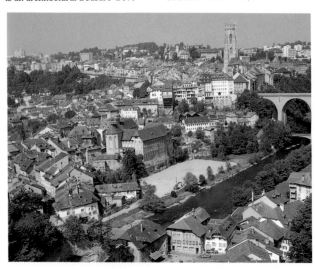

college, numerous institutes and seminaries, a conservatory of music and a well-endowed library confer upon Fribourg an intellectual task of universal dimensions.

A good place to begin a visit is from the **Chapelle de Lorette**. Following the steep road descending from this vantage point, the visitor passes by the Capuchin **Convent of Montorge** and the Cistercian **Abbey of Maigrauge**. The perspective then narrows as the modern-day pilgrim enters the town itself, with its narrow, delicately curved streets and stairways, flanked by Gothic façades.

Cathedral

Heading towards the heart of the town, the way now leads upwards towards the Cathédrale Saint-Nicholas and the Bourg quarter. Witness to six centuries of history, the collegiate church, having become a cathedral when Fribourg was elevated to a bishopric, contains masterpieces in stained glass (Mehoffer 1905 and Manessier 1980) as well as a renowned organ built by Aloys Mooser and recently restored.

Museums

The **Musée d'Art et d'Histoire** (Museum of Art and History), in the elegant Renaissance Hôtel Ratzé, 227 rue Pierre-Aeby, is one of the most visited in Switzerland. In addition to numerous expositions of classical and modern art of international stature, it contains manifold collections exemplifying both local and national history and art, extending from prehistoric times to the present day. Its extension into the house known as the 'Abbatoir' (a one-time slaughterhouse) enables visitors to admire major sculptures of the Middle Ages.

Open: daily except Mondays.

The **Figurentheatermuseum** (Puppet Theatre Museum), is situated in the old town at 2 Derrière les Jardins. The **Beer Museum** in the Cardinal Brewery offers free tastings. To arrange a visit telephone: (037) 821151

Open: Sundays; also Fridays and Saturdays in July and August.

Hotels, Restaurants and Winebars

Recommended hotels include the **Hôtel de la Rose**, 179 place Notre Dame, and the **Hôtel Duc Berthold**, 112 rue des Bouchers.

There are over 50 restaurants: the **Buffet de la Gare** is a bustling traditional French-style brasserie. The **Marmite**, in the Duc Berthold, is one of the more exclusive venues in town.

Sports

There is an ice-skating rink, indoor swimming pool, tennis courts, horse-riding, an 18-hole golf course seven miles away. Other activities include sculling and rowing on **Schiffenen Lake**, and even gliding, flying or short air excursions from the regional airport at **Ecuvillens**.

Tourist Office: Square les Places CH-1700 Fribourg (tel: (037) 813175)

◆◆◆ (summer)
◆◆◆ (winter)
GENEVE (GENEVA) ✓

Framed by the Alps and Jura mountains, Genève is located on the shores of the largest of the Alpine lakes: **Lac Léman** (Lake Geneva). Lakeside promenades and parks with flower beds and unexpected statues are all typical of this city, while the magnificent lake creates a leisure-resort atmosphere, an impression enhanced by the *mouettes*, or water taxis, which carry passengers from shore to shore, and by the larger boats inviting the visitor to longer lake trips. The **Jet d'Eau**, a towering spray of water over the lake, is Genève's landmark, seen from afar during summer.

The Jet d'Eau forms a gleaming column against the lights of Genève

Built on both sides of the Rhône, it is a major hub of European cultural life, an important venue for international meetings, a popular centre for conventions and exhibitions, and a major financial, commercial and industrial city. Yet thanks to its lively, cosmopolitan atmosphere, its wealth of museums, parks, excellent hotels and restaurants, it also attracts more visitors each year than any other Swiss city – and has refined the art of looking after them to a high degree.

Lower Town
The lower town, which lies between the south bank of the

Rhône and the old town, is the city's main business and shopping quarter, containing rue du Rhône and other smart shopping streets such as rue de la Corraterie. In place Neuve are three of Genève's landmarks: the **Grand-Théâtre, Conservatoire de Musique**, and the **Musée Rath** with art exhibitions (open daily).

Old Town

Don't miss the old town, with its art galleries, antique shops, book stores and typical bistros. Dominated by the **Cathédrale de Saint-Pierre** (St Peter's Cathedral) the real centre is the place du Bourg-de-Four, considered the oldest square in the city, dating back to Roman times. From an archaeological standpoint the new excavations under the cathedral are internationally important. The site dates from AD1000 and has yielded much evidence of early Christian life and art.

The cathedral was constructed in the 12th century under the Bishop de Faucigny. Built in a mixture of Romanesque and Gothic styles, it was completed in less than 60 years. The chapel to the right of the cathedral's main entrance is known as '**La Chapelle des Macchabées**' and was built in flamboyant Gothic style by the Cardinal Jean de Bogny in the 15th century.

Over the centuries the cathedral – which was called 'St Pierre' from the outset – was ravaged by fire and rebuilt on several occasions. The most important change took place in 1756 when a portico in Graeco-Roman style was added to hide the damage caused to the face by the weather, and the cathedral's wooden steeple, which had burnt down, was replaced by the present metal one.

The **Hôtel de Ville** (town hall), not far from the cathedral in Grand-rue, is also part of Genève's old quarter. Here you find the authorities representing the republic and the canton of Genève. The façade of this rather austere building was begun in 1617 and finished only at the end of the 17th century, a third floor being added at the beginning of the 19th century. It contains a vast and elegant courtyard with a ramp leading up to each floor. It is the site of the founding of the International Red Cross in 1864.

Next to the town hall, on the esplanade known as La Treille, is a large square tower built in the latter half of the 15th century and known as the **Tour Baudet** after the former name of its locality.

Opposite, on the other side of the street, is the former **arsenal** built in the first half of the 17th century for use as a granary and cereal market.

The **Maison Tavel**, which faces it on the rue du Puits-Saint-Pierre, is one of the old town's most interesting buildings. It was built in the 12th century and partially rebuilt in the 14th century.

Parks and Gardens

Genève is rightly proud of its spacious parks with their fountains, sculptures, bandstands and cafés. Among the best are the **Jardin Anglais** on the left bank, notable for its flower clock; and the **Parc de la Grange**, with a beautiful rose garden, the site of the annual international competition of new roses.

Museums

There are 30 museums in Genève. The **Musée d'Art et d'Histoire** (Museum of Art and History) at 2 rue Charles-Galland, houses valuable Egyptian, Greek and Roman works of art, a coin collection and an exhibition of Swiss furniture.
Open: daily.
The **Musée de l'Horlogerie** (Watch and Clock Museum), at 15 route de Malagnou, has a rare collection of 16th- 20th-century enamelled, decorative clocks, watches and music boxes.
Open: daily.
The **Musée d'Instruments Anciens de Musique** (Museum

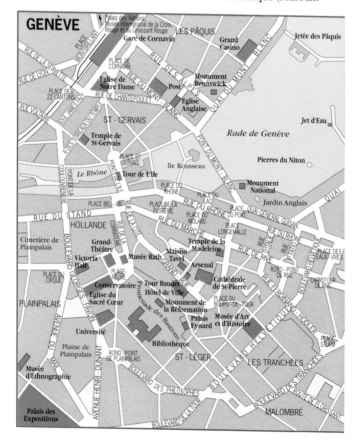

of Old Musical Instruments) at 23 rue François Le-Fort, houses a varied collection of musical instruments from the 16th and 19th centuries.
Open: Tuesdays, Thursdays and Fridays.

Accommodation

The **De La Paix**, 11 quai du Mont-Blanc, is stylish, comfortable and with an outstanding reputation, as is its near-neighbour, **Le Richemond** at jardin Brunswick. In the moderate price bracket, try the **California Hotel** at 1 rue Gevray, whose roof garden is a delight in summer. The **Beau-Rivage**, quai du Mont Blanc is in the best tradition of Swiss hotels, closely rivalled by near-neighbours, the **Bristol**.

Entertainment

The **Grand-Théâtre** is one of the most opulent opera houses in Europe, while the Victoria Hall is home of the celebrated **Orchestre de la Suisse Romande**. Nightlife centres around Place du Bourg-de-Four, and particularly recommended are the cabaret/music halls **Maxim's**, **Griffin's Club** and **Pub Clemence**.

Restaurants

There is an excellent fixed-price menu at **La Mère Royaume**, and the **Au Fin Bec** has a long-standing reputation for traditional Swiss dishes.

Shopping

If you have a bottomless purse you can have a field day in **Genève**, noted for its exquisite jewellery and watches.

Excursions

Numerous excursions are possible from Genève, thanks to its excellent location and transport facilities. One of the most popular is to the small French town of **Divonne**, located about 11 miles (18kms) away. This is noted for its thermal baths and also for its gambling casino.
Summer visitors can also enjoy horse-racing and sailing in the resort.

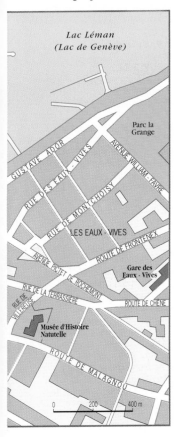

*Lac Léman
(Lac de Genève)*

Parc la Grange

GUSTAVE - ADOR

RUE DES EAUX - VIVES

AVENUE WILLIAM - FAVRE

RUE DE MONTCHOISY

LES EAUX - VIVES

ROUTE DE FRONTENEX

AVENUE PICTET DE ROCHEMONT

Gare des Eaux - Vives

RUE DE LA TERRASSIÈRE

RUE DE VILLEREUSE

ROUTE DE CHÊNE

Musée d'Histoire Natutelle

ROUTE DE MALAGNOU

0   200   400 m

Lac Léman Region

Surrounded by steep sloping vineyards, Lac Léman is the centre of sports and recreation activity for residents and visitors alike. Above the vineyards forests abound, with the Alps forming a dramatic backdrop across the lake.

Steamers offer trips along the lake during the summer months. The most popular is the special tour to see the palatial homes of international film stars and business magnates which line the shores. Mont Blanc, Europe's tallest mountain, can be seen in the distance.

Thanks to the Alps which tower above it to the east and the Jura which bounds it to the west in the direction of France, the Lac Léman region has always offered outstanding opportunities for winter visitors. The Vaudois Alps, whose resorts have been constantly modernised over the years, have nevertheless remained faithful to the well-established traditions that have gained them the enviable reputation they still enjoy.

Château d'Oex, a mainly family resort (see page 69), Les Mosses straddling the pass of the same name, Les Diablerets with its picturesque charm, Leysin with its youthful ambience and finally Villars with its elegant appeal, are all names that have contributed to the success of Swiss tourism. These resorts offer countless possibilities not only to beginners and average skiers but also to those who enjoy runs requiring a high level of skill. Cross-country skiers have not been forgotten either, and many tracks have been prepared for them through the sort of unspoilt mountain scenery dreamed of by nature lovers.

Useful Addresses

Tourist Office: 1 Tour-de-l'Ile, CH-1211 Genève 11 (tel: 022 287233)

Information: Gare Cornavin, CH-1201 Genève (tel: 022 455200)

Hospital: 24 rue Micheli-du-Crest (tel: 022 469211/226111)

◆◆ (summer)
◆ (winter)

GRUYERES

The historic, medieval village, is a quaint, picturesque place with one cobblestoned street, a fountain in the centre and rows of Gothic and Renaissance houses (protected against change by a national trust), shops, restaurants and hotels. Most vehicles are banned to preserve the streets and allow more strolling area.

At the end of the main street is the 12th-century **Château** that housed the counts of Gruyères up to the 16th century. It is now owned by the state and is open to the public. Visitors can tour its rooms, filled with displays of period pieces. *Open*: daily.

In the castle and around the town you will notice the symbol of the counts of Gruyères – a crane (*grue* in French).

The **fromagerie** or dairy of Guyères, located at the train depot of the same name, is two hours from Genève. Each day the local farmers collectively bring their milk to this modern facility where it is processed into Switzerland's famous Gruyères cheese. Though the plant is modernised with the latest technological machinery, the cheese itself is still made in the age-old tradition.

The step-by-step process is explained in Italian, French, German and English for the convenience of visitors. Samples of the product are offered in the café adjacent to the dairy, where visitors can also buy snacks and gifts.

Hotels
Both the **Hostellerie St-Georges** and the **Hôtel de Ville** provide comfortable accommodation in historic surroundings.

Tourist Office: CH-1661 Pringy (tel: 029 61036)

◆◆◆ (summer)
◆◆◆ (winter)
LAUSANNE ✓

Lausanne, which lies about half way along the north bank of **Lac Léman**, has a strongly individual

Gruyères, famous for its cheese, is a beautifully preserved medieval town

charm, immediately arresting and inviting, but not to be enjoyed without a little effort – from Ouchy on the lakeside to the highest point of the city is a stiff climb of about 770 feet (235m). There is a convenient little railway running from the city centre (place St François) down to Ouchy, the city's port. There is a permanent holiday mood at Ouchy, where young and old throng the pavement cafés drinking wine, strolling round the boat quays or settling down to a first-class meal in one of the many restaurants. It is here too, that the Lac Léman steamers come alongside, and where sailing boats can be hired. The successors of the inhabitants of Roman Lousonna gradually moved from the lakeside up the slopes, settling in places which could be better defended. On these ridges, where the Cité now stands, arose the **Bishop's Palace** (housing a museum with exhibits of old Lausanne) and the stately **Notre Dame Cathedral**, consecrated in 1275 by Emperor Rudolf von Habsburg and Pope Gregory X. One of the finest Gothic buildings in the country, it is one of the last places in the world to still have the tradition of the night watch. The hours from 22.00 hours until 02.00 hours are called out by a watchman looking out over the city.

At the end of the 14th century and the beginning of the 15th, the bishops built **Château St Maire**, which is now used as the seat of the canton government. Around this nucleus grew the modern city. Today, bridges link the various parts of Lausanne: Grand Pont, Pont-Bessières and Pont-Chaudro. Above and below the bridges are houses which often cling so closely to the hillsides that they have entrances on several levels.

Museums

The **Palais de Rumine** (Rumine Palace), built at the beginning of this century, houses Lausanne University and several museums covering fine arts, history, natural history and botany. *Open*: Tuesday to Sunday.

The **Musée Olympique** (Olympic Museum) at 18 avenue Ruchonnet, traces the history of the Olympic Games. *Open*: daily. Sunday and Monday, afternoon only.

Festivals and Fairs

The headquarters of the Federal Court, the International committee for the Olympic Games and the many international fairs and congresses have given Lausanne an international reputation. Many of the exhibitions and other events take place in the **Palais de Beaulieu** where there is also one of the biggest and most modern of Switzerland's theatres. And it is here that every year from May to July for the past 24 years, well-known artists of the world of music and dance have gathered together. Lausanne puts on its happiest and most hospitable face during the last week of June for the city festival.

Hotels and Restaurants

There are several really excellent hotels in Lausanne, the

Flower-seller in Lausanne. The town is a lively and cultured centre for French-speaking Switzerland

Beau-Rivage Palace being probably the best of all, set in a large park on the shores of the lake in Ouchy.

The **Girardet**, in the **Hotel de Ville** is so renowned that diners are asked to book months in advance for dinner. Also good are **La Grappe d'Or** at 3 rue Cheneau-de-Bourg, The **Café Beau-Rivage** in the hotel of the same name, and **La Voile d'Or** in Vidy. For delicious pastries, you should try the **Café Manuel** in place St François.

Shopping

Many first-class stores are found along the rue St François and the rue du Bourg. Good buys are watches and jewellery, leather goods and chocolates.

Excursions

There is a fascinating military museum in the nearby small town of **Morges**, containing weapons and uniforms dating from the early 16th century, as well as the Museum Alexis Forel with an important collection of dolls, toys and games.
Open: daily.

At **Nyon** a popular summer resort flanking the lake, the 13th-century castle is now a historical and porcelain museum. *Open*: daily, April–October.

Tourist Office: 2 avenue de Rhodanie, CH-1000 Lausanne (tel: 021 6177321)

◆◆ (summer)
◆◆◆ (winter)
LES DIABLERETS
The holiday resort of Les Diablerets is situated some 3,900 feet (1,200m) above sea-level in the very heart of the Vaudois Alps at the foot of a mountain range capped by a breathtaking glacier. Parallel development of agriculture and tourism is one of the characteristics of this mountain village which dates from the Middle Ages, and which today offers the visitor a wide choice of accommodation in hotels, rented apartments, and chalets. In summer Les Diablerets is the starting point for many walks or hikes across an extensive nature reserve, with a wide network of marked paths. An excursion to the **Diablerets glacier** is a very special experience. It takes an aerial cable car only 35 minutes to reach the glacier at 9,800 feet (3,000m) above sea-level, where the snow never melts and where visitors can often enjoy summer skiing or set off for walks and mountain tours. There are also guided trips on a snow-bus across the glacier. To complete its wide range of activities, Les Diablerets can also offer sports such as mountain climbing, tennis, swimming, fishing in mountain streams and lakes, rafting, riding, miniature golf, and an 18-hole golf course near by.

Hotels
Les Lilas is one of the best hotels in Les Diablerets, with an attractive dining room that enjoys a high reputation for the standard of its cuisine. **Hôtel Les**

The mountains around Les Diablerets

Diablotins offers less expensive accommodation in a mountain setting.

Tourist Office: Case postale 42, Bâtiment BCV, CH-1856 Les Diablerets (tel: 025 531358)

◆◆ (summer)
◆◆◆ (winter)
LEYSIN

Located in the Vaudois Alps, Leysin is one of the most delightful mountain resorts in Switzerland, known for its refreshing, invigorating and sunny climate, its attractive surroundings, and its superb Alpine panoramas.

The history of this international health resort dates back to 1890 when the sleepy mountain village was discovered by famous doctors and became known worldwide as a centre for treating lung and bone diseases. Huge sanatoria and hotels were built, but after World War II the sanatoria gradually emptied.

In the 1950s the focus in Leysin shifted from being a mountain health resort to becoming a leisure resort. Today, those seeking rest and relaxation, nature-lovers or those interested in active sports, can choose from a wide range of activities and facilities in both summer and winter.

For summer visitors there is an extensive network of marked paths throughout the whole region: climbing courses are offered by the Leysin mountaineering school; and there are gondola lifts to take visitors to the **Mayen Alp** or to the **Berneuse** peak where they can enjoy a magnificent view from the Bernese Alps to the Mont-Blanc massif. Coach excursions to the Diablerets glacier, Montreux or Genève are readily available.

There are indoor or open air facilities and centres for such sports as tennis, table tennis, squash, indoor golf, miniature golf, swimming, fishing, riding, hang-gliding and skating. And at **Aigle**, some 20 minutes away, there is an 18-hole golf course. In winter, Leysin offers excellent skiing for beginners and intermediates. There are two main cable cars, La Berneuse and Mayen, plus numerous ski or chairlifts and several nursery slopes.

Hotels and Restaurants

Among the best hotels are the **Hôtel Central-Residence**, **Le Relais-Regency** and the **Mont-Riant**. The restaurant **Le Leysin** specialises in dishes *au feu de bois* (cooked in a wood-fire oven).

Entertainment

Leysin is more suited to families and those who are happy with quiet evenings rather than to swinging visitors who like to dance the night away.

Tourist Office: CH-1854 Leysin (tel: 025 342244)

◆◆◆ (summer)
◆◆◆ (winter)
MONTREUX ✓

Since the 18th-century writer Jean-Jacques Rousseau chose the Montreux area as the setting for his novel *La Nouvelle Héloise*, the town has developed into one of

the most popular and populated places on **Lac Léman**. Its geographical position is superb, being on a wide bay, open to the south, with wooded hills and sloping vineyards to the rear protecting the whole area from north and east winds. The lake stores the heat, reflects the light, and makes Montreux's climate delightful.

It is the mildest area north of the Alps with an average annual temperature of 10°C (50°F), to which the extraordinary vegetation bears witness. There is a wealth of trees and plants, some of them subtropical, on the *quais* – a paradise for strollers – between Clarens and Chillon Castle. Fig and almond trees flourish, as do laurels and eucalyptus; there are cypresses, magnolias and palm trees, and

Montreux, on the shore of Lac Léman, is a romantic sight at nightfall

every spring the whole town resembles a huge bouquet, with its higher-lying pastures covered with thousands of narcissi.

Present-day Montreux developed out of 20 former hamlets. Apart from its wide modern streets there is also an old quarter with picturesque alleys located higher up the slopes. And those who venture still higher can enjoy an enchanting panorama from Glion, Caux, Les Avants or Sonloup.

Lake and mountains – and the carefully tended parks in the town, where one can sit and enjoy the view – are an invitation to rest and relaxation.

Although Montreux retains a handful of luxury hotels belonging to a past era, many modern hotels and buildings show that the town is not prepared to rest on its laurels. And thanks to its wide range of hotels, offering a total of 4,000 beds, its conference and exhibition centre and its casino, Montreux is increasingly becoming a meeting place for people from all four corners of the globe.

Château de Chillon (Chillon Castle)

One of Montreux's chief attractions, and one of the best preserved medieval castles in Europe, is the beautiful 13th-century Chillon Castle. Immortalised by Lord Byron in his poem *The Prisoner of Chillon*, this one-time prison stands on a rock promontory jutting into the lake, south of the town. *Open*: daily.

Festivals

In spring there is the Golden Rose (Rose d'Or) international television competition and rock festival; in July, the Jazz Festival; in September, the Classical Music Festival, to mention but a few local events. Popular local festivals, and other cultural activities help to ensure that there is always something going on for visitors to enjoy.

Hotels

Of the luxury hotels the **Montreux Palace**, 100 Grand-rue, and **Grand Hotel Excelsior**, 21 rue Bon Port, are world famous, and the first class **Suisse et Majestic**, 43 avenue

des Alpes, with its traditionally styled bedrooms, some overlooking the lake, can also be recommended. Of the moderately priced hotels the **Helvétie**, 32 avenue du Casino, is extremely good, with a pleasant roof terrace.

Restaurants

The **Restaurant Francais** of the **Suisse et Majestic** hotel, with its attractive furnishings and excellent cuisine is popular. Any of the three restaurants in the classy **Hotel Eden au Lac** are also recommended.

Excursions

There are mountain railways to transport the visitor into a wonderland of sights and experiences; on **Rochers-de-Naye**, 6,700 feet (2,042m) above sea-level, the restaurant **Plein Roc** built into the rock face offers a stunning view; and the Montreux-Bernese Oberland Railway offers excursions to such places as **Château D'Oex** and **Gstaad** (see pages 69 and 37).

Tourist Office: 5 Rue de Theatre, CH-1820 Montreux (tel: 021 9631212)

◆◆ (summer)
◆ (winter)
NEUCHATEL
Neuchâtel, a charming town located on the edge of its lake (Lake Neuchâtel) and at the foot of Chaumont, has much to interest the visitor, including the 12th-century Collegiate Church, the castle (mainly 15th- and 16th-century), and the old part of town with its ancient fountains and patrician houses. In addition

it has museums (see below), an excellent library and an active cultural life thanks to its being a university town.

The countryside and lakeshore bordering Neuchâtel provide ample scope for relaxation and walking. Here you will find picturesque villages and old fortified towns such as **Grandson**, vineyards, fields and woods, beaches, swimming pools, castles and museums, as well as facilities for nautical sports, fishing and camping. **Yverdon-les-Bains**, a well-known spa resort, offers what is said to be the biggest outdoor thermal pool in Switzerland.

Museums

The **Musée d'Art et d'Histoire** (Art and History Museum) contains a large collection of French Impressionist works, plus a world-famous collection of music boxes and automated dolls. A demonstration of the music boxes takes place the first Sunday in each month.
Open: daily except Mondays.
The **Musée Cantonal d'Archéologie** (Archaeological Museum) has many exhibits found in local caves dating back 50,000 years.
Open: Tuesday to Sunday, afternoons only.

Hotels and Restaurants

The **Beaulac**, overlooking the lake is the best in town. The **Marché** is central and excellent value. Of the numerous restaurants, the **Aux Vieux Vapeur**, converted from an old lake steamer, is fun, and serves delicious fish. For mouth-watering pastries there is **Wodey-Suchard**.

Excursions

There are popular excursions to **Chaumont** and to the **Jura heights**, or you can cruise on the three Jurassian lakes. **St Ursanne** on the River Doubs, **Porrentruy** in the Ajoie, and **Delémont** with its prince-bishop's castle, all have architectural treasures.

Tourist Office: 7 rue Place-d'Armes, CH-2001 Neuchâtel (tel:(038) 254242)

◆◆ (summer)
◆◆ (winter)
VEVEY

Vevey, on Lac Léman, is a 'Swiss Riviera' resort with an interesting history, having been at the crossroads of Europe since the Roman Empire. It prospered as trade expanded in the Middle Ages and further progressed on the arrival of the French Huguenots. Tourists began discovering its attractions in the 19th century.

Charlie Chaplin in Vevey; the town hosts a comedy film festival

The lakeside promenade, which extends for more than 5½ miles (9km), is noted for its lovingly tended flower beds. And Lac Léman also provides Vevey visitors with a wide range of watersports and cruising opportunities.

Every Monday and Saturday the Vevey marketplace comes alive with an exhilarating open market, which often includes local wine tastings. Roughly four times a century (next in 1999), Vevey celebrates a 'Winegrowers' Festival' (*Fête des Vignerons*) which includes a huge wine pageant with thousands of people participating.

The resort is also a mecca for musicians and film-makers; it is the venue for the Clara Haskil piano competition and the International Comedy Film Festival; and together with Montreux is host to the annual Montreux-Vevey Music Festival.

Museums

Together with wine and tourism, chocolate is Vevey's other mainstay. The famous Nestlé corporation has its headquarters here and the **Alimentarium** (Museum of Nutrition) at 1 rue du Léman was founded by the company. It covers the natural science, ethnography and history of food.

Open: Tuesday to Friday.

Also of interest is the **Musée Suisse d'Appareils Photographiques** (Swiss Museum of Cameras) at 4 Grande Place, a collection of cameras from the late 19th century to the present.

Open: Tuesday to Friday.

Mont Pèlerin

A 10-minute ride by funicular or car up to Mont-Pèlerin, a region of woods, farms and villas, is highly recommended. The view from here is considered by many to be one of the best in Switzerland, taking in Lac Léman, Vevey, Montreux, The Rhône Valley and the French Alps. You can, if you wish, return to the lakeside on foot, visiting the picturesque medieval village of **Chardonne** on the way.

Hotels and Restaurants

Leading hotel of Vevey is the **Trois Couronnes**, 49 rue d'Italie, beautifully situated overlooking the lake and which was the setting for the film Daisy Miller. Among the best restaurants are **Chez Pierre**, and **Restaurant du Rivage** with its idyllic lakeside terrace.

Excursions

Vevey is a good starting point for excursions. The range is wide: a leisurely drive among the vineyards; a variety of short or long boat trips on the lake; a cogwheel train ride to soak up the mountain scenery along the way to **Gstaad**; or panoramic views from **Les Pléiades** or **Rochers-de-Naye**.

Tourist Office: Grand Place 29 Gare, CH-1800 Vevey (tel: (021) 9214825)

◆◆ (summer)
◆◆◆ (winter)
VILLARS

At 4,265 feet (1,300m) above sea-level on a plateau high above the Rhône valley, and commanding a superb panoramic view of the Vaudois Alps, the Valaisan Alps, and Mont Blanc, Villars is one of Switzerland's premier winter resorts – and one of the best equipped.

In summer too there is plenty to do. For walkers there are 186 miles (300km) of marked paths, and excursions are organised on which the visitor can enjoy a view of the whole Alpine chain, for example by taking an aerial cable car to the **Roc d'Orsay** at 6,500 feet (2,000m). In Villars itself the New Sporting leisure club offers squash and tennis courts, volley ball, badminton, a Turkish bath and an amazing, electronically controlled 18-hole golf course simulator. Other resort facilities include indoor and outdoor swimming pools, an ice-skating rink, miniature golf, and a real 18-hole golf course.

Summer visitors to Villars can enjoy the outdoor swimming pool

There are also facilities for bowling, parachuting and fishing in mountain lakes as well as a fitness club and circuit. Tennis and golf tournaments are held in summer, as are table-tennis and petanque competitions.

In winter the resort offers 75 miles (120km) of prepared pistes, ranging from gentle nursery slopes to the 9,800-foot (3,000m) high glacier at **Les Diablerets** (see page 80), linked to the Villars ski region. Other winter activities include cross-country skiing, ice-skating and delightful mountain walks along the many well-marked footpaths.

The ancient spa town of **Bex** (pronounced 'Bey'), a short drive down the valley, is well worth a visit.

Hotels

The four-star **Panorama Hotel** is well run and nicely furnished, with facilities that include a heated swimming pool, sauna, solarium, lounge, spacious bar and sun terrace.

The **Hôtel Marie-Louise**, situated in the village centre, is a charming family-run hotel furnished in traditional Swiss style.

Entertainment

There are several discos such as the **El Gringo** and the **Copernic**, while **Uncle Sam** at the **Panorama Hotel** has a lively disco and live entertainment from time to time. **Peppino's** also has live music and dancing.

Tourist Office: CH-1884 Villars-sur-Ollon (tel: 025 353232)

LIECHTENSTEIN

The royal residence of Vaduz Castle

With Switzerland to its west and south and Austria to its east lies Liechtenstein, tiny, independent and extremely prosperous. Liechtenstein has been around since 1719, when the domain of Schellenberg and the county of Vaduz were welded into an independent principality – a little gem of a country just over 15 miles (25km) long and 3¾ miles (6km) wide. With not quite 30,000 inhabitants occupying a total area of 62 square miles (160sq km), it is a microscopic geographical unit; yet despite being so tiny it is divided politically into an upper region – once the county of **Vaduz** – and a lower region, formerly the domain of **Schellenberg**. It comprises a total of 11 autonomous communities which together offer an extensive range of attractions – museums, boutiques, hotels, restaurants, historical sites, vineyards and plenty of sports facilities – but at the same time retains its own very individual charm and appeal.

Liechtenstein is also a family-oriented place, with adventure playgrounds to keep children happy. There are exhibitions, amateur theatre productions, folklore and intellectually stimulating concerts, while the **Theater am Kirchplatz** in Schaan presents entertainment of every kind – films, ballet, pop singers, plays and children's theatre, clowns and dramatised fairy tales.

◆◆ (summer)
◆ (winter)
VADUZ
As one might expect, the biggest community, Vaduz, is the capital and also the main tourist centre. Located close to the right shore of the Rhein at the foot of the

mighty Rätikon peak, it was once a village primarily known for its excellent wine, but has developed into a busy capital with industry, banks, offices and service industries. It is dominated by Vaduz castle, the prince's residence built around 1300. The castle is not open to the public.

Art Collection

A main attraction for visitors is the Art Gallery housed in the Englanderbau at Städtle 37. The works are chiefly from the collection of the Princes of Liechtenstein – one of the oldest and most comprehensive private collections in Europe. Peter Paul Rubens' subtle portraits of his children by his first marriage are exhibited, as well as his monumental cycle of paintings of the Roman Consul, Decius Mus.
Open: daily.

National Museum

Those interested in natural history and the history of civilisation will enjoy the **Liechtensteinisches Landesmuseum** at Städtle 43. Items exhibited include historical finds from excavations in the principality, church carvings, old coins and selected items from the private arms collection of the ruling prince.
Open: daily except Mondays in winter.

Postmuseum

Liechtenstein's postage stamps, tiny works of art featuring scenes of the countryside and reproductions of paintings in the royal art collection, are highly regarded by philatelists throughout the world. The Postage Stamp Museum, Stadtle 37, has a large collection of the most distinctive Liechtenstein stamps dating back to 1912. Entrance free.
Open: daily.

Mountain Walks

Depending on mood and physical condition, you can stroll alongside a swirling mountain brook with the family, grill sausages over an open fire and, after a snooze, help the children build a dam across the brook; or you can follow reliably marked footpaths through the romantic valleys, up across sun-drenched terraces into the seclusion of the Alps. The famous **Furstensteig**, a marked footpath starting from Gaflei, offers marvellous views over the Rhine Valley. The little resort of Malbun also provides excellent mountain walks.

Formalities

There are no customs formalities on the Liechtenstein-Swiss border. Such formalities do exist, however, on the border to Austria's federal state of Vorarlberg north of Liechtenstein. Entry and customs regulations are the same as for Switzerland.

Hotels and Restaurants

Vaduz offers 340 beds in nine hotels and inns, mainly small establishments. The youth hostel Schaan/Vaduz, with 80 beds, is located between Vaduz and Schaan.

Liechtenstein National Tourist Office, Städtle 37, PO Box 139, FL-9490 Vaduz (tel: 075 2321443)

PEACE AND QUIET

Wildlife and Countryside in Switzerland
by Paul Sterry

The visitor to Switzerland is confronted with natural beauty at every turn. From the imposing, snow-covered peaks of the Eiger or the Jungfrau to immense glaciers eroding Alpine valleys and the dazzling array of colour to be found in the flower-rich meadows, there is always something of interest. Scenic beauty is not confined to the uplands of the Alps and the Jura, however; the low lying land between the mountain ranges, studded with tranquil lakes and lush pastures, provides a peaceful contrast. The distribution of Switzerland's wildlife is strongly linked to altitude, some species preferring lowland areas and others found only on the highest peaks. Being able to recognise elevation by the vegetation, therefore, will help the visitor to know what species to look for. Because of Switzerland's excellent system of roads, funicular railways and skilifts, the visitor can easily see all the altitudinal habitats, from lowland deciduous forests through mountain slopes covered with spruce to the snow-covered peaks above the tree line. And this can all be done in a single day.

Towns, Parks and Gardens

Without venturing far you can often enjoy a surprising variety of wildlife, and in particular several species of birds. If staying in the mountains, alpine species may be seen, especially during the winter when they descend to the lower slopes, while at lower altitudes, the species tend to be those otherwise found on the edges of woodland.

Swifts

One of the most familiar summer sounds in small Swiss towns is that of screaming swifts. Parties of these most aerobatic birds skim through the streets at breakneck speed uttering their shrill call. Nests are built under eaves and in the roofs of houses, and this species is seldom found breeding away from human dwellings. Its larger relative, the alpine swift, is a comparatively rare visitor to towns, preferring to nest on rocky cliffs, but is nevertheless found in a few towns at higher altitudes.

In western Europe, hawfinches are generally secretive woodland birds, but in Switzerland, as in many other countries further east, they seems to cohabit with man quite successfully and are often seen in parks and gardens with mature trees. The reverse is the case with the robin, however, which is a familiar garden bird in some countries, but in Switzerland is a shy bird found only in natural woodland. In Swiss gardens, its place is taken by another superficially similar bird, the black redstart. Also found among boulders and scree on mountainsides, this charming little bird often nests in outhouses and old walls.

Mature parks in the vacinity of woodland may attract red squirrels which sometimes approach people for food, and the lowlands are also the haunt of familiar birds such as

PEACE AND QUIET

Goldfinches feed on seed heads

blackbirds, great tits and greenfinches. Where rough ground supplies a source of seeds, tree sparrows and goldfinches may also be found and before long the calls of collared doves, a comparatively recent addition to Swiss gardens, will be heard. Having spread from eastern Europe several decades ago, they are now widespread throughout most of western Europe. Spring sees the arrival of a more proficient songster: the serin. Like its cage-bird relative, the canary, the male has a delightful twittering song.

Lowland Valleys and Agricultural Land

Despite the dominance of the Alps and the mountains of the Jura, a considerable part of Switzerland is comparatively low-lying, being under 3,000 feet (900m) above sea level. Separating these two ranges is the Mittelland which runs from the Bodensee (Lake Constance) in the east to Lac Léman (Lake Geneva) in the west. Many of the rolling hills and valleys have been given over to agriculture and this charming region also contains much of the country's human population.

Flower-rich grazing meadows are a colourful sight, with a wealth of flowers of many species. Precisely which species are found depends upon the time of year and the nature of the soil. The altitude at which the meadow is found is also an important factor and at moderate elevations, giant yellow-green spikes of false helleborine dominate the scene. Grasslands buzz with the sound of insects in summer, and colourful butterflies flit from flower to flower. Grasshoppers and crickets scurry among the vegetation and many fall victim to the hovering kestrels or great grey shrikes, which use fence posts and overhead wires as vantage points. These same perches are often used by corn buntings, whose buzzing song, which is supposed to resemble jangling keys, is a familiar sound of the lowland Swiss countryside. The closely related cirl bunting, whose yellow and chestnut markings make it more elegant than the drabber corn bunting, is also found locally. Sunny south-facing slopes, particularly around the shores of Lac Léman, often have vineyards which are the haunt of red-backed shrikes and ortolan buntings. The former often sit on prominent perches, ever alert for passing insects, while the latter are more secretive and creep along furrows in the ground. Keen-eyed observers may spot a diminutive little owl perched on a post or branch, but Scop's owls, although present, are seldom seen because they are extremely well camouflaged. After dark, however, their monotonous, whistling call soon gives their presence away, although it is still almost impossible to locate them.

Lakes, Rivers and Freshwater

Throughout the low-lying Mittelland region to the north of the Alps is found a range of freshwater habitats. Rivers draining water from the mountains feed immense lakes such as Lac Léman and Lakes Constance, Neuchâtel and Zurich. These lakes are rich in wildlife, but with increasing pressure from land reclamation and development, man has had a profound influence on many of these habitats, seldom improving the environment for wildlife. Artificial reservoirs, such as the Klingnauer Reservoir, are, however, an exception and have actually created a new habitat for water birds.

Wherever a river feeds or drains one of the large, natural lakes, a small delta often forms. Exposed shingle ridges sometimes have breeding little ringed plovers, and water plants, reedbeds and wet woodland add to the diversity. The sanctuary that this provides is a haven for breeding birds such as cots, mallards, little grebes and water rails as well as many, less numerous species such as red-crested pochard, black-necked grebe and garganey. Great crested grebes also nest here, and in early spring, pairs can be seen performing their elaborate courtship displays on the open water, each partner holding water plants in its beak. Springtime sees the arrival of many migrant birds from south of the Mediterranean which come to breed in the tangled, waterside vegetation. Reed, great reed and Savi's warblers sometimes sing from exposed perches and find the abundant supply of insects such as midges, caddis flies and mayflies richly repays their journey north. The warblers construct neatly woven nests among the reed stems, but their skills at construction are slight by comparison with penduline tits, whose bottle-shaped nests are suspended from the tips of twigs. The waters of many of the lakes have large populations of fish and amphibians, which in turn feed many species of bird: little bitterns and grey herons silently stalk the shallows and black kites scavenge any remains they leave.

Migrant waders pass through the Mittelland region, and species such as wood sandpiper, Temminck's stint and spotted redshank feed along open shores or where exposed mudbanks permit. Although many waders can be seen in spring, their numbers and the variety of species in autumn makes this a more rewarding time for the birdwatcher.

PEACE AND QUIET

Deciduous Forest

Thanks to strict Swiss forestry laws, the foothills of the Alps and the Jura are still, in part, cloaked in woodland. At these comparatively low elevations, both the tree species of the woodlands and the wildlife they contain differ markedly from the higher altitude spruce forests: here the trees are mostly deciduous, especially beech, possibly interspersed with conifers, and these forests hold a wide range of woodland birds and mammals.

Pure stands of beech support only a limited range of plants and animals when compared to more mixed woodlands. The leaf canopy is so dense that only the most shade-tolerant plants can grow on the woodland floor. However, a careful search during the summer months may reveal helleborines or the curious bird's-nest orchid in the deepest shade, while clearings may hold small clumps of mezereon, adorned with pink flowers in spring and red berries in autumn.

In spring, beech woodlands come alive with the song of wood warblers, often accompanied by chiffchaffs and Bonelli's warblers in clearings and rides. Great spotted and black woodpeckers, also found in most other types of woodland in Switzerland, are most easily seen here in spring. Where a variety of tree species occurs, marsh tits, firecrests and even golden orioles may be found. The latter's fluty song is marvellously evocative of the tropics and carries far on a still morning. Birdwatchers who like a challenge should try identifying treecreepers and short-toed treecreepers, both of which are found in Swiss woodlands. Birds seen only briefly can often defy identification, but with a more prolonged view the whiter flanks of the treecreeper may be discerned.

Around farms, the woodland has often been cleared to create grazing pastures. This effectively increases the woodland edge which often allows better views of wildlife than the woodland interior, and the patchwork landscape is particularly favoured by grey-headed woodpeckers and pied flycatchers, while roe deer may occasionally venture into the open to graze. Although the mixed woodlands have quite a few mammals, these are generally rather difficult

to see. Polecats, pine martens and foxes are all found, but are rather wary of man; red squirrels, on the other hand, can sometimes become quite approachable.

Upland Forests
Ascending the wooded mountain slopes, the visitor will notice the forest gradually changing in appearance. Increasing altitude brings with it a decrease in air temperature and greater threat from heavy winter snows, so less hardy lowland species of tree, such as beech, are gradually replaced by conifers. At their most characteristic, these upland forests comprise mainly spruce, but larch is often present as well.

As the appearance of the forest

Yellow wood violets - flower gems which grace many Swiss woodlands

changes, the wildlife it contains also changes. Although birds such as black woodpecker and great spotted woodpecker appear to thrive in almost any forest of reasonable size in Switzerland, the increase in altitude brings with it an interesting addition. The three-toed woodpecker, recognisable by its black-and-white striped face, is markedly upland in its distribution. It is the only species of woodpecker likely to be encountered in Switzerland which shows a white rump in flight.

Nutcrackers are common and are often seen perched on the tops of trees, while in the lower branches, redpolls, crested tits, and willow tits all forage for insects.

Towards the upper limit of the forests, known as the tree line, the birdwatcher will begin to encounter citril finches. These delightful little yellow-green birds build neat nests among the branches of the conifers and sometimes descend to lower altitudes outside the breeding season. Tengmalm's and pygmy owls are seldom seen except by chance, and eagle owls, despite their immense size, are wary and secretive. Equally large, the capercaillies which lurk in the forests are sometimes disturbed by ramblers from among piles of fallen branches. They are Europe's largest gamebird. Their smaller relative, the hazelhen, although quiet and unobtrusive in habits, is comparatively less timid and if spotted will sometimes sit motionless, staring back at the observer.

PEACE AND QUIET

Above the Tree Line

Once the exclusive realm of their animal inhabitants and a few intrepid climbers, the highest reaches of many of Switzerland's most threatening and imposing peaks now yield their secrets to large numbers of visitors. Roads, funicular railways and skilifts from centres such as Zermatt, Interlaken or Grindelwald - and even a railway through the heart of the Eiger - allow easy access to many slopes and summits in both summer and winter. As with many human endeavours, however, these activities bring both benefits and costs and, in places, the pressure of human visitors is causing soil erosion and snow compaction, leading to a deterioration in the majestic environment they come to visit.

Spring gentians in an Alpine meadow

Above an altitude of about 6,000 feet (1,800m) the trees become stunted and gradually disappear to be replaced by areas of low scrub and scree and boulder fields. At the highest elevations, glaciers and permanent snow fields dominate the landscape, but right up to their edge, creeping and low-growing vegetation, such as mosses, dwarf willows, saxifrages and sandworts, persists. Where the soil is sufficiently loose, alpine marmots dig their burrows and form loose colonies, and among the boulders, rock thrushes, rock partridges and ptarmigan feed and make their nests.

Along tracks and paths, alpine accentors and snow finches search for insects and seeds and are sometimes almost indifferent to the presence of people.

Rocky outcrops are also the haunt of chamois, sure-footedly crossing gulleys and rock faces which would cause the pulses of most climbers to race. The most magnificent creature of all, however, is the ibex. Small colonies of these wild goats, such as that at Piz Albris, still survive despite former persecution.

The skies high above the peaks are the domain of golden eagles and peregrine falcons, and the occasional griffon vulture drifts by, ever alert for casualties of this inhospitable terrain. Ravens, easily identified by their wedge shaped tails and loud 'cronking' calls, sometimes mob these birds of prey if they pass too close to the raven's territory. Their relative, the alpine chough, is much more numerous in the skies above the mountains. Flocks of these engaging birds wheel and turn, their finger-like wing feathers giving them great agility. Like other members of the crow family, they are quick to learn and have taken to accosting human visitors for food.

Alpine Meadows

If the Alps are the scenic glory of Switzerland then the Alpine meadows must surely be its botanical highlight. Against the backdrop of snow-clad peaks, these meadows, grazed by cattle during the summer months, are a riot of colour from May until August and, to anyone who has ever seen them, a lasting memory.

Daisies, knapweeds, bellflowers and hay-rattles grow in profusion, and in wet hollows, clumps of butterworts,

louseworts and marsh marigold add to the variety. Here and there among the commoner species, those with a keen eye may spot the orchids which also thrive in these pastures. Burnt orchids and the creamy-white spikes of the elder-flowered orchids are widespread, favouring meadows where the underlying soil is limestone. Between June and August, the meadows are graced by two particularly elegant species, the round-headed orchid and the black vanilla orchid, flowers of the latter having a noticeable smell of vanilla.

Alpine meadows often echo with the sound of a loud, whistling call, the source of which is not a bird but a mammal, and a very curious one at that. Alpine marmots are large rodents with course fur which live in burrows among tussocks of grass. Although they often become indifferent to the presence of man, they remain ever alert for predators such as the golden eagle and the shrill alarm call serves to alert fellow marmots.

Specialised Alpine Flowers

Above the tree line, the scree slopes and boulder fields are the highest habitats to support plant life before the domain of permanent snow and ice is reached. For flowering plants, these peaks are among the most inhospitable places on earth, with air temperatures that can quickly plummet below freezing, even during the summer months and, to add to their problems, for at least six months of the year they are likely to be covered with a thick blanket of snow. This layer is both a blessing and a curse to the ground flora: it insulates the plants from the worst excesses of the winter blizzards but it also effectively cuts off the light. Despite the rigours of the environment, however, the spring and summer bring about a transformation in the landscape with alpine plants bursting into an array of colour that would be the envy of any gardener with an alpine rockery.

With the snows often not thawing until April or May and reappearing again often as early as September, plants have a short growing season in which to flower and produce seeds and build up stores for the coming winter. Many do not even wait until the snow has cleared completely and the charming, nodding flowers of the alpine snowbell push their way through the melting snow. These are followed shortly after by hardy crocuses and several species of gentians, the most attractive of which is perhaps the spring gentian, whose blue flowers stud the vegetation. White flowers of sandworts and pearlworts seem to grow out of bare rock and a careful search of short turf may even reveal the diminutive false musk orchid. Unlike its more showy relatives, which are found at lower elevations in the Alpine meadows, this plant has a rather grass-like appearance and is barely 1¼ inches (3cm) high. The flowers that grow in the true alpine zone (ie above the tree line) are extremely specialised and thrive here because they do

not have to compete with the lush vegetation found in the lowlands. Although many are dwarfed or creeping, thus avoiding the fierce, biting winds, and are rather slow-growing, some are more showy. The alpenrose, which despite its name is a dwarf species of *Rhododendron*, is one of the most attractive, its rose-coloured flowers adorning the low-growing bushes, but its less showy companion, edelweiss, is the best-known alpine species.

Switzerland's Alpine Butterflies

With all this variety of flowers it is not surprising that insect life is also abundant. Despite the altitude and often considerable daily temperature fluctuations, butterflies are numerous. Blues, skippers, fritillaries and whites all look attractive as they flit between the flower heads in search of nectar, but none can compare with the most elegant of Alpine butterflies, the apollo. Its flight is rather leisurely and from certain angles the wings look like brilliant fragments of stained glass. Like the Greek god after which they were named, apollos are true sun-worshippers, only taking to the wing when the sun shines. On dull days and at dawn and dusk they sit on flower heads in a state of lethargy, often allowing the observer, or the photographer, to get to within inches of them.

Winter Wildlife

Although many animals either hibernate or migrate to escape

An inquisitive alpine chough

the winter, some remain active throughout the year. When weather conditions are particularly harsh, some are lured close to human habitation so that, in many places, visitors can observe Alpine wildlife while indulging in their favourite winter sport.

Many of the animals at home in the highest reaches of the Swiss mountains descend to lower altitudes during the winter months, when snow covers their summer feeding grounds, making the search for food either difficult or impossible. Snow finches and alpine accentors inconspicuously search for seeds and hibernating insects among rocks and vegetation and often feed close to skilifts.

The disturbance caused by the human visitors does not seem to upset them unduly, and they may even benefit where trampling feet clear areas of snow. On occasions, they even join inquisitive and bold alpine choughs around restaurants and cafes and take food from visitors.

Elegant and sure-footed chamois haunt rocky outcrops and stand out conspicuously if seen against a blanket of snow. Ptarmigan, on the other hand, have plumage which varies according to the season and blend in with their natural surroundings. The white winter feathers match the snow and help the bird avoid detection by golden eagles who patrol the skies above. This seasonal change in appearance is not confined to the bird world and 'ermine' stoats are often seen by skiers. When in hot pursuit of a small mammal, they seem to lose all fear of people and scamper in the open.

Switzerland's wildlife interest in the winter is not confined to the mountain slopes and many of the country's larger lakes, such

PEACE AND QUIET

as Lakes Constance and Neuchâtel, are important wintering sites for waterbirds, mainly because they almost invariably remain ice-free. Lac Léman, which is the largest lake in western Europe, is one of the most important of such sites and estimates of between 50,000 and 100,000 coots, gulls and ducks (in particular tufted duck and pochard) are usual. Goldeneye and goosander are commonly seen and are sometimes joined by divers and grebes, more usually associated with the marine environment at this time of year.

The diversity of species found on Lac Léman is at least partly attributable to the variety in habitats around its margins, which vary from open shore to reedbeds and woodland. The abundance of many species, however, is thought to be related to the presence of the introduced zebra mussel, an excellent source of food for hungry birds.

The Forest of Deborence

Situated in Val Triqueut, northwest of Sion, the Forest of Deborence reserve contains some of the finest alpine habitats in Switzerland. In particular, the fir woodlands are thought to be the last truly virgin areas of forest left in the country, but rocky slopes and Alpine meadows are also richly rewarding.

Search long enough in the forest and you should come across crested tits, black woodpeckers and three-toed woodpeckers among the mature trees, while fortunate observers may see a fox. Hazelhens are present, but, as elsewhere, they are difficult to see since they blend in with their surroundings so well. Black grouse also occur and where pastures adjoin the woodland, or in secluded woodland rides, early morning hikers may stumble across a 'lek' of males, each one competing with the others for the attention of a female. Chamois, rock buntings and small parties of rock partridge are found around rocky outcrops and scree slopes, and where these form inaccessible cliff faces, eagle owls may nest. Remaining motionless throughout the day, these magnificent birds, with an immense wingspan, can sometimes be found by scanning with binoculars. Higher up on the rock faces there may even be a golden eagle's eyrie - a very exciting discovery!

Purple coltsfoot in a forest glade

Shaded rock faces are often dripping with ferns and mosses which appreciate the moisture than runs over the surface. These primitive plants harbour insects and spiders which, in turn, provide food for one of the Alps most curious and delightful birds. Wallcreepers could not be more aptly named since this is exactly what they do. No rock face is too sheer for them and they skilfully search out invertebrates in the cracks and crevices with their long downcurved beaks. Their flight is rather moth-like as they glide on rounded, purple wings, tipped with black and white. At the base of the cliffs small streams often form and the damp environment is much to the liking of alpine salamanders. Although salamanders generally remain hidden under stones until nightfall, they are often found foraging during the day after recent rainfall.

A migrant honey buzzard

Migration through the Alps

To migratory birds, who each year journey to and from their breeding territories in northern Europe and their wintering grounds in southern Europe or Africa, the Alps present a tremendous obstacle. The weather is often hazardous and considerable energy is expended in attaining sufficient height to fly over the mountains. Not surprisingly, therefore, most birds choose the line of least resistance and fly through one of the passes which for the birdwatcher, has the effect of concentrating the migrants and providing a rich spectacle at the right times of year.

In spring; during April and May and more especially in the autumn from late August until October, birds of prey and passerine migrants fly through in their thousands. Passes such as Bretolet and Cou are widely considered to be the best spots, but their comparative inaccessibility often deters visitors. Any of the other passes through which roads or funicular railways run may be equally rewarding on certain days, and the sight of hundreds of buzzards, honey buzzards, swallows and martins, together with smaller numbers of hobbies and finches, is a memorable sight.

FOOD AND DRINK

Switzerland has no lack of good restaurants offering a wide choice of specialities. There is not really any such thing as Swiss cuisine, only regional foods and dishes which are nourishing, wholesome, and often country-style. Specialities include Neuchâtel tripe; *Berner Platte*, a Bernese dish of boiled meat and sausages served with haricot beans; *Rösti*, grated fried potatoes; St Gallen sausages (*Bratwurst*); *papet* from the canton of Vaud (leeks with potatoes); Ticinese *risotto*; Basel's brown-flour soup (*Mehlsuppe*) and onion flans; Zürich's shredded veal (*schnitzeltes Kalbfleisch*); barley

A typical hearty meal in one of the many waterfront restaurants which combine eating with a view

soup and air-dried meats (*Bundnerfleisch*) from the Grisons; and of course all the cheeses – Gruyére (*Greyerze* in German and Groviera in Italian), Emmentaler, Appenzeller, Jura, the French-Swiss *tommes*, and the herb cheeses from Eastern Switzerland, plus the famous cheese dishes *fondue*, *raclette* and cheese flans.

Nor should the visitor overlook the many fish dishes, the endless varieties of bread, the red and white wine specially chosen to go with each of these dishes, the range of spirits, Kirsch, Williamine, marc and grappa, and finally the ciders and mineral waters.

Then there are the cakes and confectionery: *cuchaules* and *taillaules* (breads eaten on Sundays), butter cakes and *bricelets* from the

FOOD AND DRINK/SHOPPING/ACCOMMODATION

French-speaking part of Switzerland, Kirsch gâteau from Zug, Unterwalden's scrambled pancakes, pear bread from central Switzerland, carrot gâteau from Aargau, *Leckerli* honey biscuits from Basel, Bernese meringues, and nut cake from the Grisons.

Menus

It is important to note that the 'menu' is *Karte* in German-speaking Switzerland and *carte* in the French-speaking part. If you ask for a 'menu' the waiter is more likely to return with the dish of the day, since that is what the word means to the Swiss. All *Karten* have a menu, which is usually the chef's special at a moderate price; this may also be listed as *Tagesplatte*, *Tagesteller* or *plat du jour*, depending on whether the language is German or French.

Wines and Spirits

Switzerland has eight wine areas and as many vintners as there are sunny slopes for growing grapes. The major areas are Genève (red and white wines), Neuchâtel and Vaud (white), the southern Valais (white Fendant and red Dôle), the Ticino (red Merlot), and Graubünden (red Veltliner). Fruit brandies are a popular Swiss speciality.

Swiss Chocolates

As well as the famous names of Tobler, Nestlé and Lindt & Sprüngli, look out for the products of gourmet chocolatiers such as Moreau, found in the Neuchâtel region, and Zurich-based Teuscher.

SHOPPING

Switzerland's superb products make it a shopper's paradise. Fine watches come in an infinite variety. More good buys are textiles, embroideries, fine handkerchiefs, woollen sportswear, and linen. Chocolates come in an amazing variety of sizes, shapes and flavours. Other good buys include precision instruments, drafting sets, multi-blade pocket knives, music boxes, woodcarvings, ceramics and other handmade items, antiques and art books.

Generally shops are open from 08.00/09.00 hrs until 18.30 hrs from Monday to Friday and 08.00/09.00 hrs until 16.00/17.00 hrs on Saturday. In large towns some shops may close Monday mornings, while in suburban areas and small towns, shops normally close on Wednesday or Thursday afternoon. In some areas shops may close for lunch.

ACCOMMODATION

Hotels

Swiss hotels are the envy of hoteliers throughout the world, and understandably so in view of their exceptionally high standards, both in terms of accommodation and service. The Swiss Hotel Association (SHA, Schweizer Hotelier-Verein, Monbijoustrasse 130, CH-3001, Bern, tel: (031) 507111) publishes a yearly guide of 2,680 hotels and pensions which are members. The guide shows the rates, addresses, telephone/telex numbers, opening dates and amenities of the various hotels.

The SHA also publishes a list of hotels that offer special terms for senior citizens, mostly between the main holiday seasons. In addition, the *Swiss Hotel Guide for the Disabled* contains details about hotels for guests confined to a wheelchair (see **Disabled Travellers** and **Senior Citizens** sections in the **Directory**). These guides are all available from the Swiss National Tourist Office. A list of hotels and restaurants catering for Jewish visitors can also be obtained from the SNTO.

The SNTO does not make hotel reservations, however. Visitors are therefore advised to book direct with the hotel or through a travel agent or hotel representative. Those wishing to make advance reservations may obtain advice on arrival at local tourist offices, during business hours. Some main railway stations and airports have hotel reservation facilities.

Chalets and Apartments

Information regarding the rental of chalets, houses and furnished apartments for holidays is available from local tourist offices and estate agents in Switzerland. A list of contacts is available from the SNTO.

Youth Hostels

Youth hostel accommodation is available to visitors up to the age of 25 years. Hostellers over 25 admitted if there is room. Visitors from abroad must hold a membership card of their national organisation affiliated to the International Youth Hostels Federation. To avoid disappointment, wardens of youth hostels should be given prior notice (at least five days) of arrival. The SNTO publishes a list of Swiss Youth Hostels. The local association is: Schweizerischer Bund für Jungendherbergen (Swiss Youth Hostel Association), Neufeldstrasse 9, CH-3012 Bern 22 (tel: (031) 245503).

CULTURE, ENTERTAINMENT, NIGHTLIFE

Entertainment

Entertainment opportunities in Switzerland are boundless. Whatever the season the visitor will encounter festivals, folklore performances, concerts and the like both during the day and evening. In all the principal ski resorts there is always something happening after the day's sport, including lively discothèques and night-clubs which continue into the small hours. The same applies to the major cities and towns, even though the Swiss are not by nature night owls – hardly surprising since most of them start work at 07.00 hours! However, the early start certainly does not deter them from joining in the fun of the many carnivals staged throughout the country, such as that in Basel in February, or in the lively celebrations marking Swiss National Day on 1 August. Generally speaking, the concert and theatre season runs from September to May, but in summer, music festivals are organised by several Swiss cities – the most prestigious of which is the one held in Luzern.

Jazz lovers will not be disappointed either, especially if they are in Montreux in the summer for the annual festival. Lists of events including art exhibitions, music festivals, folklore programmes and sporting events are obtainable from SNTO.

Gambling

Gambling in Switzerland is restricted to boule, and the maximum stake that can be placed is Sfr 5.

WEATHER AND WHEN TO GO

The conditions vary considerably and no country in Europe combines within so small an area such marked climatic contrasts. In the northern plateau surrounded by mountains, the climate is mild and refreshing; south of the Alps it is warmer, coming as it does under the influence of the Mediterranean; while the Valais area is noted for dryness. In winter, high mountain slopes can be sunny and warmer than the valleys.

All can join in the fun of carnival, and plenty such events take place, particularly at Mardi Gras

Daily weather reports covering about 25 resorts are displayed in all major Swiss railway stations and outside post offices in holiday resorts.

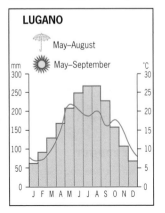

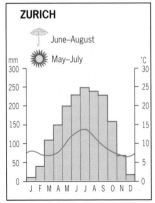

HOW TO BE A LOCAL

Correctness and reliability are key Swiss characteristics. Buses run on time – to the second; laws are diligently observed; and fairness and quality are highly valued. Switzerland is not a showy place, and the Swiss reserve can give an initial impression of coldness. But you will find that, behind this restraint, there lies a diverse and welcoming society. Since the Swiss enjoy one of the highest standards of living in the world, experiencing Switzerland as the locals do inevitably implies having a healthy sufficiency of funds at your disposal. But even those Swiss on limited budgets can make the most of the good things this country offers: by avoiding, for instance, except on very special occasions, the restaurants, cafés and bars enjoying the best locations, and patronising instead the smaller establishments found away from the main tourist haunts; by opting for the excellent public transport rather than expensive taxis; and by enjoying the various – free – carnivals, street processions and folklore events.

PERSONAL PRIORITIES

Female visitors to Switzerland – including those travelling independently – should encounter few problems. In some of the remoter mountain villages and the staunchly Roman Catholic Ticino region, single women on their own are sometimes regarded with slight suspicion, but generally speaking Switzerland is a safe and welcoming country for all visitors. Unwanted sexual advances by locals, for instance, are extremely rare: it is fellow visitors that the female traveller should be on her guard against. Hardly surprisingly, in view of its huge pharmaceutical industry, all leading legal drugs are available in Switzerlands' pharmacies. Not all are readily available over the counter and, as in the UK, pharmacists will require a prescription from a Swiss-registered medical practitioner.

CHILDREN

Switzerland is a wonderful holiday destination for children and youngsters, and the Swiss have refined the art of looking after their needs and preferences. Apart from the many and varied facilities for winter sports for which expert tuition is readily available, children can also choose from a vast range of year-round sports opportunities, from excellent swimming pools and skating rinks to tennis courts and miniature golf courses. They will also delight in the numerous festivals, carnivals, processions and folklore events held in towns and villages throughout the country – some of them accompanied by spectacular firework displays – while even small toddlers are well catered for at supervised kindergartens in all the major holiday resorts.

TIGHT BUDGET

One way of keeping costs down while visiting Switzerland is to avoid staying in the most

Learning to ski can be an exciting experience for active youngsters

popular and fashionable resorts, choosing, instead, the small hotels and guest houses in neighbouring villages where prices are considerably cheaper. 'Einfach & Gemütlich' (Simple and Cosy) is a voluntary chain of family-run small hotels, pensions, dormitories and mountain lodges, all in the most reasonable price category. There are 175 hotels in 143 locations, many off the beaten track, listed in the *E&G Hotel Guide* which is available (charge) from the SNTO. Cheap accommodation can often be found in private houses. Look out for the sign 'Zimmer' (in German-speaking Switzerland where most of such rooms are) or 'Chambres á louer' in French-speaking regions. In summer, efficiently-run camping sites are found near every major tourist centre. (see **Directory** page 110).

Swiss public transport is excellent, so you should not experience much difficulty finding your way to the more up-market resorts. It is worth buying one of the various cost-saving transport cards and passes widely available (see **Directory** pages 119–22).

SPECIAL EVENTS

January

Folk celebrations in most towns and villages to usher in the New Year; horse-racing on snow in St Moritz and Arosa; the *Vogel Gryff* festival in Basel; International Lauberhorn ski races in Wengen.

February

Famous Basel carnival, beginning on the Monday after Ash Wednesday; *Fritschi* festival in Luzern, beginning the Thursday before Ash Wednesday; procession of harlequins in Schwyz; *Mardi Gras* in the Ticino; speed skating championships in Davos.

March

Engadine cross-country ski marathon; Parsenn Derby downhill ski race at Davos; footwashing ceremonies on Maundy Thursday in numerous Catholic communities; religious processions in many southern towns on Good Friday.

April

Festa delle Camelie at Locarno; *Sechseläuten* festival of Zürich, featuring a parade and bonfire; blessing of horses, donkeys and mules at Tourtemagne on 23 April; start of the *Primavera Concertistica* classical music festival in Lugano.

May

Festival of the *Feuillu* on the first Sunday in May at Catigny, Genève; procession headed by the Grenadiers of God at Kippel, in the Valais, Spring Musical Festival in Neuchâtel; beginning of festival of music and ballet in Lausanne; Golden Rose Television Festival at Montreux.

June

Rose Week in Genève; International June Festival in Zürich; Art Festival in Bern; High Alpine ballooning at Mürren.

July

Rose Festival of Weggis; crossbow shooting in the Emmental; giant slalom on the Diablerets' glacier and summer ski race on the Jungfraujoch; International Jazz Festival of Montreux; Nyon Folk Music Festival.

August

Swiss National Day celebrations throughout the country on 1 August, with firework displays a feature; Genève Festival, featuring fireworks and parades; music festival in Luzern and film festival in Locarno; folk festivals at Interlaken; Yehudi Menuhin festival at Gstaad.

September

Shooting contest in Zürich; torchlight religious processions at Einsiedeln; music festival in Montreux (also at the end of August and beginning of October).

October

Garden show in Genève; agricultural and dairy show at St Gallen; Italian Opera Festival in Lausanne; vintage festivals in wine-growing regions.

November

Numerous open-air markets throughout Switzerland, that at Bern, the Zibelemârit (onion market), with public festivities, being one of the most fascinating.

December

World-famous ice hockey tournament in Davos; *Escalade*, an ancient custom, in Genève on 11 and 12 December, with torchlight processions; numerous festivals on St Nicholas Day, 6 December.

SPORT

Winter sports are, of course, the main activities sought by visitors to Switzerland. For information on facilities available see page 10 and entries for individual resorts. However, there are also plenty of other ways of using up energy.

Cycling Bicycles can be hired from Swiss Federal Railway stations and some of the private railway administrations.

Advance reservations should be made directly to the station booking office.

Fishing In Switzerland's countless streams, rivers and lakes the angler will find plenty of exciting sport. Restocking of lake, brook, brown and rainbow trout as well as grayling and pike is done every year. As the fishing regulations vary from one place to another, it is best to enquire about licences and regulations at the hotel or local tourist offices.

Hiking Local walking and excursion maps are obtainable at the tourist offices of most resorts, and Ordnance Survey maps can be ordered through the Swiss National Tourist Office. Suggestions for eight walking tours across Switzerland are included in a leaflet *Walking Tours in Switzerland* and obtainable from the SNTO.

Mountaineering The most

The invigorating air and varied scenery make hiking a constant joy on any visit to Switzerland.

SPORT

challenging peaks of the entire Alpine region are in Switzerland. In summer, as in winter, they offer many attractive goals to which access has been facilitated by some 150 mountain huts which various branches of the Swiss Alpine Club have built.

You can learn the intricacies of the technique of mountain climbing at the mountaineering schools in Andermatt, Champéry, Les Collons, Davos, Les Diablerets, Disentis, Engelberg, Fiesch, La Fouly, Glarus, Grindelwald, Kandersteg, Klosters, Meiringen, Pontresina, Raron, Riederalp, Saas-Fee, Saas-Grund, Sils (Engadine), Thun, Urnâsch, Verbier and Zermatt. Guides are also available at many other resorts.

It is important to remember, however, that excellent physical condition and appropriate equipment are essential, and that on no account should a climb be attempted without a guide.

Tennis/Squash There is hardly a Swiss resort without tennis courts (some indoors) and squash courts. Many hotels maintain their own courts.

Watersports Opportunities for swimming are found at all altitudes. Lidos have been established by lakes and rivers, and numerous indoor and outdoor artificial pools have been built for the enjoyment of holidaymakers. Most bathing lidos are open from June until September, even longer in warmer regions. Many hotels also have heated swimming pools open throughout the year.

Swimming has a special appeal against the backdrop of Swiss mountains

DIRECTORY

Contents

Arriving

By Air

The Swiss airlines Swissair and Crossair fly to Switzerland from more than 110 cities in 70 different countries. Switzerland has four intercontinental airports – Zürich-Kloten, Genève-Cointrin, Bern-Belp and Basel-Mulhouse. All have the usual large airport facilities including duty-free shops, car rental desks and money exchange facilities. It is easy to travel to all parts of the country from Zürich and Genève airports, which are directly linked into the excellent Swiss rail network, making it easy to reach many destinations. Trains run to and from Zürich main station at least every 20 minutes, the journey taking 10 minutes. Regular trains link Genève airport with Cornavin station, a six-minute journey. Basel has an airport coach service to the city centre, as also has Genève.

Fly-Rail Baggage Passengers arriving in Switzerland by air via Zürich, Basel or Genève airports can check-in their baggage from the airport of origin and have it transported through to their Swiss destination. Customs declaration forms and the baggage labels can be bought from the SNTO. Homegoing air travellers whose flights are booked from Basel, Zürich or Genève airports can check their luggage through to their final destination from many Swiss towns and resorts. A charge of Sfr 20 per item of luggage is made for this service. With a rail ticket the charge is less than if the luggage alone is sent. Full details are given in a 'Fly-Rail' leaflet published by the SNTO.

By Rail

There are several rail routes across Europe to Swiss cities. The EuroCity Express 'Loreley' runs from Hook of Holland to Basel, Lugano and Chiasso. Another EuroCity train 'Edelweiss' covers the route from Brussels to Basel. From Paris there are high-speed TGV *(Train à Grande Vitesse)* services to Genève, Lausanne and Bern. Advance booking is necessary for most of these journeys. Contact the Swiss National Tourist Office for more details.

By Road

Visitors can take a private car, towed caravan, motorcycle or motor scooter into Switzerland for a temporary stay without customs documents provided a valid national driving licence – which should be carried at all times – and the vehicle registration certificate can be produced.

For information on travelling within Switzerland, see **Driving** (page 112) and **Public Transport** (page 119).

Entry Formalities

A valid passport (or, in the case of British travellers, also a British Visitor's Passport) is essential for entry to Switzerland. Holiday or business visitors to Switzerland or Liechtenstein do not require a visa if they are holders of a valid national passport from Australia, Canada, Eire, Great Britain and the United States of America (as well as many other countries), and are intending to stay for a period of no more than three months.

Camping and Caravanning

There are approximately 600 camp sites in Switzerland, and camping guides are published by the Swiss Camping and Caravanning Federation (Schweizerischer Camping-und Caravaning-Verband, Habsburgerstrasse 35, CH-6004 Luzern , tel: (041) 234822) and the Swiss Camping Association (Verband Schweizer Campings, Seestrasse 119, CH-3800 Interlaken, (tel: (036) 233523). The season extends from April/May to September/

October, though some sites are open all year.

Chemists see Pharmacists

Crime

The Swiss are, on the whole, a law-abiding people. However, it is always wise to take precautions when on holiday, especially when it comes to protecting your valuables and possessions. Those staying in ski chalets, for instance, should be extra careful about leaving money or expensive items of jewellery lying around. Even in the big cities it is sensible to deposit valuables in hotel safes.

Customs Regulations
Importation

Visitors may generally temporarily import the following goods into Switzerland free of duty and other taxes: personal effects such as clothing, toilet articles, sports gear, photographic and amateur cine cameras with appropriate films, video equipment, musical instruments, and camping equipment; food provisions (including soft drinks) up to the quantities a person normally requires for one day; other goods declared on crossing the border and imported for gift purposes (with the exception of meat and meat preparations which are covered by special regulations, butter and quantities of goods, intended to be laid in store), provided their total value does not exceed Sfr 200. Visitors aged under 17 are entitled to half this limit.

Alcoholic beverages and tobacco may be imported in the following quantities:

	Visitors from	
	European countries	Non-European countries
Alcoholic beverages:		
– up to 15 degrees	2 litres	2 litres
– over 15 degrees	1 litre	1 litre
Tobacco:		
– Cigarettes	200	200
– or Cigarillos	100	100
– or Cigars	50	50
– or Pipe Tobacco	250 grammes	250 grammes

The exemption from alcohol and tobacco duty applies only to persons of at least 17 years of age.

Road vehicles and boats. Road vehicles and boats temporarily imported for personal use do not require a customs document for up to one *year* in the case of a vehicle and one *month* for a boat. However, they do require an adequate third-party insurance policy, valid for Switzerland. Boats must also bear a sign of the canton on whose waters they are to be used for the first time.

Exportation
The exportation of certain items from Switzerland may be prohibited or restricted by the import regulations of the country of your destination. Before returning home or visiting any other country outside Switzerland you should familiarise yourself with the customs regulations of that country. There are no restrictions on the import or export of foreign or Swiss currency.

Disabled Travellers
Two organisations that can supply information for disabled travellers are the Swiss Invalid Association (Schweizerischer Invalidenverband Froburgstrasse 4, CH-4601 Olten) and the Swiss Study and Working Group for Disabled Persons (Schweizerische Arbeitsgemeinschaft für Körperbehinderte, Feldeggstrasse 72, PO Box 129, CH-8032 Zürich). Brochures available cover holiday apartments, holiday hints for the disabled and motels, camping and caravan sites, restaurants, rest houses and toilets along Swiss motorways accessible to wheelchair users. There are also lists of excursion resorts and aerial cableways fulfilling the requirements for disabled persons and of transportation facilities for the disabled.

Hotels
The Schweizerischer Invalidenverband in conjunction with the Swiss Hotel Association, also publishes a hotel guide for the disabled. It categorises hotels according to ease of access for wheelchair users and includes details of door widths, accessibility of restaurants and suitability of

DIRECTORY

Hotels at 'the village of the glaciers', Grindelwald

toilets and lifts. The hotel guide is available from the SNTO or from the Schweizerischer Invalidenverband.

Driving
The minimum age for driving in Switzerland is 18 years, although car rental companies reserve the right to set a higher minimum age, and invariably do so (see below under **Car Rental**). For motorcycles (exceeding 125cc) the minimum age is 20 years.

Breakdown
The emergency number for summoning assistance in the event of a car breakdown is 140. There are SOS telephones along all motorways and mountain passes.
If you are a member of an affiliated club in your own country, the major motoring club, Touring Club Suisse (TCS) operates a 24-hour breakdown service which can be summoned by telephone – see below under **Motoring Organisations** for details. When calling, give the operator the password, *Touring Secours, Touring Club Suisse,* and state your location and the nature of the trouble. A patrol car or breakdown truck will come out to you, but it is likely you will be charged for any other service.

Car Rental
The major rental firms such as Avis, Budget, Europcar, Eurorent, and Hertz are all represented in Switzerland. A car can be rented from airports, most large towns, and in arrangement with Hertz – from railway stations. The minimum age for driving a rented car is

20 to 25 years (depending on the company) and a valid National or International Driving Licence (held for at least a year) is required. Rates include third-party insurance but collision insurance (an extra charge), is recommended.

Documents
A valid driving licence and the vehicle's registration papers are the only documents needed if you want to drive your own car in Switzerland. For insurance, it is recommended that a Green Card be obtained from the driver's insurers.

Motoring Organisations
There are two Swiss motoring associations with branch offices all over the country: the Touring Club Suisse (TCS), rue Pierre-Fatio 9, CH-1211 Genève 3 (tel: (022) 7371212); and the Automobil-Club der Schweiz (ACS), Wasserwerkgasse 39, CH-300, Bern 13 (tel: (031) 328 3111).

Motorway Tax *(Vignette)*
An annual road tax of Sfr 40, known as *Vignette* is levied on all cars and motorcycles using Swiss motorways. An additional fee of Sfr 40 applies to trailers and caravans. Permits are available at the border crossings and from post offices, garages or service stations in Switzerland and are valid for multi re-entry into Switzerland within the duration of the licence period. The *vignette* is valid between 1 December of the year preceding and 31 January of the one following the year printed on it. To avoid hold-ups

at the frontier it is advisable to buy the *vignette* in advance from Swiss National Tourist Offices or motoring clubs in your own country.

Speed Limits
On motorways, 75 mph (120 kph); other roads, unless otherwise signposted, 50 mph (80 kph); built-up areas (indicated by signs bearing the placename) and secondary roads even when not signposted, 31 mph (50 kph); caravan or trailer (up to 1 tonne) on tow, 50 mph (80 kph); and caravan or trailer (more than 1 tonne) on tow, 37 mph (60 kph).

Traffic Regulations
All (front and rear seat) passengers must wear seat belts. Children under 12 have to travel in the rear seats. Motorcyclists must wear crash-helmets. Driving with side lights only is no longer permitted under any circumstances, and the use of headlights, dipped headlights (recommended at all times for motorcyclists) or twin fog lights is compulsory. Dipped headlights are compulsory in road tunnels. A red triangle 'tunnel' sign serves as a reminder to switch on your lights.

On mountain roads a car may be asked by the driver of a yellow postal bus to reverse or otherwise manoeuvre to allow the postal bus to pass. The sound of its distinctive three-note horn often warns of the approach of a postal bus. If you are carrying luggage on a road rack the load must not exceed 50 kg for cars registered after 1 January 1980 and not over 10 per cent of the vehicle's unladen weight for cars registered before that day. Motorists should note that the laws concerning speed limits, lighting and seat belts are strictly enforced, and police are authorised to collect fines on the spot.

Weather Hazards

Because of the sometimes extreme nature of the winter climate, drivers may experience difficulties on some Swiss roads. The main highways linking the major cities are unaffected but high passes are usually closed in winter, though it is generally possible to drive within reasonable distance of all winter sports resorts. Information on weather conditions appears on notices at strategic points along roads leading up to passes. According to weather conditions, wheel chains may be required, especially at high altitudes. In these instances it is a punishable offence to drive without this equipment.

Electricity

Swiss power stations supply current at 220 volts AC. As the socket outlets require Continental-style (two 'round' pin) plugs it is advisable to carry an adaptor for the use of electric equipment, available from electrical appliance retailers, best purchased from your home country.

Embassies and Consulates

United Kingdom
Embassy
Thunstrasse 50, CH-3000 **Bern** 15 (tel: (031) 3525021).

Consulates
37-39 rue de Vermont (6th floor), CH-1211 **Genève** (tel: (022) 7343800 and 7332385). Dufourstrasse 56, CH-8008 **Zürich** (tel: (01) 2161520).

United States of America
Embassy
Jubiläumstrasse 93, CH-3005 **Bern** (tel: (031) 357711).
Consulates
Av. de la Paix 1–3, CH-1202 **Genève** (tel: (022) 7385095). Zolllikerstrasse 141, CH-8008 **Zürich** (tel: (01) 4222566).

Canada
Consulate
Kirchenfeldstrasse 88, CH-3005 **Bern** (tel: (031) 3526381).

Australia
Embassy
Alpenstrasse 29, CH-3000 **Bern** (tel: (031) 3510143).

Emergency Telephone Numbers

For Police in case of emergencies, dial 117.
For Ambulance, dial 144.
See also under **Telephones** and **Driving**.

Entertainment

In Switzerland this covers a wide range, from classical music concerts and ballet and opera performances in its larger cities to sophisticated night-clubs and lively discothèques or a cosy village *Stubli* where you can enjoy a glass of Glühwein or a beer with the locals. Après-ski life, too, varies in style and quality from resort to resort, but in all of them evening dancing and merrymaking continue well

One of the great sights of the Alps: the expanse of the Aletsch Glacier

into the small hours. At lunchtime the mountains are well supplied with spacious restaurants and little ski huts where you can sample Bratwurst sausages, Rosti potatoes, spaghetti, country soups or steak, together with the local wine or beer. Most mountain resorts have a large terrace where you can take a lunch or relax with a drink under the warm Alpine sun.

For those who like to gamble, casinos can be found in a number of cities and resorts, including Arosa, Baden, Bern Brunnen, Crans, Davos, Engelberg, Geneva, Interlaken, Locarno, Lugano, Luzern, Montreux, St Moritz, Thun and Zürich (see also page 103).

Health
Precautions

At the time of publication, vaccination and inoculation is not required by visitors entering Switzerland from European countries and the Western hemisphere. However, the situation can change, and it is always best to check with your local medical practitioner. As there is no state medical health service in Switzerland, and as medical treatment must be paid for - and is expensive - it is essential to take out insurance cover against personal accident and sickness, as well as loss or damage to luggage and personal effects and cancellation charges. Special winter sports policies are widely available.

Health Resorts

People have been going to Switzerland for centuries to seek healing in mountain air and sunshine, at medicinal springs or at the hands of specially trained doctors and nurses. The Swiss Hotel Guide lists climatic resorts according to geographical and climatological situation and indicates the disorders that are treated there.

There are 250 mineral springs in the country as a whole, each with its own properties and effects.

The best known spas are: Andeer, Baden-Ennetbaden, Bad Passugg, Bad Ragaz-Valens, Bad Schinznach, Bad Scuol, Bad Tarasp-Vulpera, Breiten, Lavey-les-Bains, Lenk, Leukerbad, Lostorf Bad, Ramsach, Rheinfelden-Mumpf, St Moritz-Bad Saillon, Schwefelberg Bad, Serneus, Stabio, Vals, Yverdon-les-Bains and Zurzach.

Holidays - Public and Religious

New Year's Day, 2 January, Epiphany, Good Friday, Easter Monday, Ascension Day, Whit Monday, National Day Christmas Day, 26 December. There are other public holidays observed in various cantons such as 1 May, Corpus Christi, and All Saints' among others.

Lost Property

If you are unlucky enough to lose something while on holiday in Switzerland you should first check with the hotel receptionist or chalet maid, and then report your loss at the nearest police station. Remember to read the clauses in your holiday insurance policy carefully to ensure you follow the correct procedures for making a subsequent claim. If you lose something on a train or bus, go to the relevant railway or public transport lost property office. The Swiss being such an honest race, the chances of recovering your misplaced article are high. However, a reward of 10 per cent of the article's value is expected by the finder.

Money Matters
Travellers' Cheques

Visitors can buy Swiss currency in the form of travellers' cheques or bank notes, from their bank, Swiss Bankers Travellers' Cheques (in Swiss francs) can be obtained from the various overseas branches of Swiss banks and many other banks. These cheques are accepted in Switzerland at their face value and without deductions.

Travellers' cheques are cashed in Switzerland by banks or by official exchange offices at airports and principal railway stations, at the current rate of exchange, less commission.

Credit/Charge Cards

The use of credit/charge cards such as Access, Visa, American Express and Diner's can be useful to supplement cash and travellers' cheques.

Swiss Currency

Notes (Swiss francs): Sfr 10, Sfr 20, Sfr 50, Sfr 100, Sfr 500, Sfr 1000. Coins (centimes or 'Rappen'/Swiss francs): 5 centimes, 10 centimes, 20 centimes, 50 centimes, Sfr 1, Sfr 2, Sfr 5.

Opening Times

Banks are open for business Monday to Friday.
Opening hours vary. For Basel the times are 08.15 to 17.00 hrs (Wednesday or Friday 18.30); Bern 08.00 to 16.30 hrs (Thursday 18.00); Geneve 08.30 to 16.30/17.30 hrs; Lausanne 08.30 to 12.00 and 13.30 to 16.30 hrs (Friday 17.00); Lugano 09.00 to 12.00/12.30 and 13.00/13.30 to 16.00 hrs; Zurich 08.15/09.00 to 16.30/17.00 hrs (Thursday 18.00).

Pharmacists open from 08.00 hrs (except Sunday). Special notices are displayed giving addresses of pharmacists on duty outside these hours.

Post offices in large towns are open from 07.30 to 12.00 and from 13.30 to 18.00 hrs. Saturday closing at 11.00 hrs except for a few major offices in cities which close later.

Shops are usually open from 08.00/09.00 till 18.30/18.45 hrs, and Saturday 09.00 till 16.00/17.00hrs, and are often closed on Monday mornings in large towns (closed Wednesday or Thursday afternoons in surburban areas).
In some cities, shops are often open once a week until 20.00hrs. The usual hours for **business** in Switzerland are 08.00 to 12.00 hrs and 14.00 to 17.00 hrs Monday to Friday.

Personal Safety

Accidents on the slopes are, unfortunately, all too frequent,

Snow always lies on the Jungfraujoch, at 11,333 feet (3,454m) above sea-level

DIRECTORY

even among experienced skiers, so it is essential to take out a good insurance policy to cover you for any eventuality. Travel companies specialising in winter sports holidays can usually provide you with suitable cover, or you can seek the advice of your local travel agent.

If you have a minor accident on the slopes requiring simple treatment, Swiss pharmacies stock a good range of medical products, and can also advise on where you can find a doctor. Sunburn is a common problem, and visitors should also be wary of being sun-blinded. Good quality sunglasses are a must. Tap-water is considered safe to drink throughout the country, but many visitors prefer to use the bottled variety which is widely available.

Grindelwald's village church

Pharmacists
Pharmacists, known variously as *Apotheke* (in German), *pharmacie* (in French) or *farmacia* (in Italian), stock a good range of medications for most complaints. The name and address of the nearest pharmacist on 24-hour duty is posted in all pharmacy windows.

Places of Worship
Switzerland is virtually equally divided between Roman Catholics and Protestants, although many other denominations are represented in the principal cities and towns. Hotel receptionists can usually be relied upon for advice on an appropriate nearby place of worship and times of masses or services. The Intercontinental Church Society offers English language services at centres in Basel (Henric Petri Strasse 26, tel: (061) 235761); and Blonay, near Vevey (1 chemin de Champsavaux, tel; (021) 9432239). Visitors from any denomination are welcome.

Police
Each Swiss canton and community is responsible for maintaining law and order within its boundaries, as a result of which police uniforms vary enormously from one place to the next. However, what they all share in common is the strict enforcement of the law combined with courtesy and the usual Swiss efficiency.

Post Office
Correspondence can be forwarded to Swiss Post Offices for collection. All envelopes

must be clearly addressed to the addressee (do not use 'Esq' or any other confusing addition), 'Poste Restante'', and the name of the town, **preceded** by the postcode. The sender's address should be marked on the back. All unclaimed mail is returned to sender if not collected within 30 days. Collection is from **main** post offices in towns. On collection the addressee is expected to produce his or her passport for identification.

Public Transport

Switzerland has an excellent public transport system, with the rail network covering all but the most remote regions, and the coaches of the Swiss Postbus Service filling the gaps. The **Official Swiss Timetable** contains full details of services and fares of the 10,000 miles (16,000km) of railway, Alpine postbuses and lake boat network, including important international connections, dining car facilities and other useful information. It is an annual publication issued at the end of May each year, and copies can be purchased from the SNTO or at any railway station in Switzerland

Rail Travel

There are trains for all tastes: express Intercity (IC) trains: fast trains: regional trains that serve the smaller stations where fast trains don't stop; rack-and-pinion trains that cling to the slopes, such as that on to Mount Pilatus or the one that climbs inside the Eiger North Face to the Jungfraujoch at 11,332 feet (3,454m); panoramic trains with turn-of-the-century carriages, such as the Montreus-Bernese Oberland line; steam traction trains like that of Blonay-Chamby in the canton of Vaud or the Amor-Express in Eastern Switzerland. And then there is the daring Glacier Express that crosses 291 bridges and goes through 91 tunnels to link St Moritz or Davos with Zermatt. To this list should be added some 400 funiculars, aerial cableways, chairlifts and even underground trains, some of which scale the highest summits. Various tickets are available for journeys within Switzerland, and it is wise to consider carefully which would be the most suitable and obtain them before travelling. Any person boarding a train without a valid ticket for the journey will be sold a single ticket with a surcharge.

Group Tickets Tickets for journeys at reduced rates are issued for groups of five or more adults. A free 'conductor' ticket is granted for a group of 15 or more fare-paying passengers.

Children's Tickets Children over six and under 16 years, who are travelling independently, travel at half-rate on Switzerland's railways, boats and Alpine postbuses. (See also **Family Tickets** below.)

Swiss Pass This entitles the holder to unlimited travel by Swiss Railways, boats and most Alpine postbuses. In addition, a reduction of 25 per cent is offered on many privately owned funiculars and mountain railways on production of the Swiss Pass. It also allows travel

DIRECTORY

on transport services of 24 Swiss towns and cities and may be combined with the family tickets in the free-travel area. You have the choice between a four-day, eight-day, 15-day or one month pass, but must be resident outside Switzerland or Liechtenstein to qualify.

Swiss Card This provides flexibility, offering travel from frontier railway stations or airports to any destination in Switzerland and back free of charge, and additional excursions by rail, bus or boat for 50 per cent of the normal cost plus reduced rates on mountain railways. Family reductions also apply. The card is valid for a month and is only available to those resident outside Switzerland and Liechtenstein.

Swiss Half-fare Travel Card This ticket enables the holder to buy, in Switzerland, an unlimited number of tickets at 50 per cent of the full fare for scheduled services of the railways (including mountain railways), postbuses and lake boats. Family reductions also apply. There are two cards, one valid for one month and the other for a year. They can be purchased from SNTO offices abroad or in Switzerland from principal railway stations.

Day Cards These entitle holders of the above Swiss Half-fare Travel Card and Swiss Pass to unlimited travel (on chosen days), on rail services shown on a map provided with the cards, and on all postbus services.

Swiss Transfer Ticket This recently introduced ticket is of particular benefit to winter sports visitors. With it, an all-in price covers the journey from frontier stations or airports to any destination in Switzerland and back, within a period of one month. Family reductions also apply.

Family Tickets For these tickets, a Family Card must be held, obtainable (free of charge) from SNTO or any Swiss Railway station. Either or both parents have to be in possession of a full-fare ticket or any of the tickets mentioned above. Children aged from six up to their 16th birthday travel free, and unmarried youngsters from 16 up to their 25th birthday travel at half-fare. The Family Card can be used for most excursions, as well as main journeys.

Regional Passes Very popular with visitors who wish to make excursions in a particular region (there are eight regions to choose from), the Regional Pass is valid for 15 days, except for the Locarno/Ascona and the Lugano areas which are valid for just seven days. The Central Switzerland region offers a choice between a seven- or 14-day pass. The 15-day pass entitles the holder to free travel anywhere within the area on five days and half-price travel for the remaining 10 days. The Locarno/Ascona and Lugano regions offer seven days' free travel. The seven-day pass for Central Switzerland offers two days' free travel. These passes are issued during the summer season only. Holders of the Swiss Half-Fare Travel Cards, Swiss Cards and Swiss Passes can obtain Regional Passes with

The old Allmendhubel funicular at Murren

a 20 per cent reduction. Pre-paid vouchers which are exchanged at the booking offices of the appropriate region, can be obtained through principal travel agents or the SNTO.

Breaks of Journey These are permitted without formality.

Luggage A 'normal' amount of luggage may be taken on trains without charge. Heavy baggage can be registered between any two railway stations and to destinations of the principal lake boat services and postbus routes. There is a standard charge per piece of luggage up to 30kg (66lbs). Special rates apply for sports equipment.

Buses

Switzerland's Postal Motor Coach service not only covers the remotest and most thinly populated corners of the land, but also offers organised excursions with or without guides. Its buses are recognisable by their bright yellow colour with a red stripe and their unmistakable 'call' - the three-note motif from Rossini's *William Tell* overture. Various transport tickets, such as special excursion and circular tickets as well as weekly passes for certain regions, allow travel at advantageous fares on the postbus services. Detailed information on these is available from the local tourist offices in Switzerland in the area in question.

On postbus routes the ticket must be officially endorsed at the start of each journey. Passengers are allowed 50kg (110lbs) of luggage free of charge.

Town Transport

Public transport in the towns is well organised. Trams, buses and funicular railways triumph over the hazards of the traffic. At some points there are park-and-ride facilities where the motorist can switch smoothly to public transport.

Pleasure Boats

Lovers of lakes are certainly not forgotten in Switzerland. Big white pleasure boats, usually with a restaurant on board, ply on all the large lakes. Paddlesteamers operate on the lakes of Brienz, Luzern, Zürich and Genève. Some stretches of the Rhein, the Rhône, the Aare and the Doubs also run boat services. Breaks of journey are permitted without formality.

Senior Citizens

Switzerland has long been a popular choice for the elderly, especially in the summer months

A lakeside promenade

when the scenery is at its most beautiful. Many of the lakeside towns offer excellent possibilities for leisurely strolls along flower-decked promenades, thoughtfully equipped with seats and benches where one can relax and admire the scenery. But elderly visitors with walking difficulties should take extra care in their choice of Swiss resort; being such a mountainous country, roads and streets can be steep and twisting.

The Swiss Hotel Association (Monbijoustrasse 130, PO Box 2657, CH-3001 Bern, tel: (031) 3704111) publishes a list of hotels offering special terms to senior citizens in the off-seasons and sometimes throughout the year. To benefit from the scheme, women must be over 62 and men over 65 (proof of age is required). Holders of an official disability pension also qualify. In the case of married couples, one spouse must fulfil the conditions. The inclusive special price covers overnight stay, breakfast, service charges, heating and taxes. Bookings (specifically referring to the scheme) can be made direct with the hotels or through a travel agent.

Student and Youth Travel

Inter-Rail is a special travel facility available to people under the age of 26 or those in possession of a valid international Student Identity Card. It involves the purchase of the 'Inter-Rail' Travel Authority Card which allows the holder to travel for one month at half-fare

on the lines of the railway issuing the card and free of charge on the lines of the other participating European Railways.

Telephones

To operate a public telephone, insert coin (or phone card) after lifting the receiver. The dialling tone is a continuous sound. Use coins to the value of 60 centimes for local calls and Sfr 1 or Sfr 5 for national and international calls. The dialling code for the UK is 00 44. Omit the initial 0 of the town code. Otherwise dial 191 for details of dialling codes when calling abroad. The cheap rate for calls is Mon-Fri 18.00-08.00 hrs; Sat and Sun all day. The following numbers can be dialled for information:
Conditions of traffic, roads and passes 163
Foreign exchange rates 160
Telegrams 110
Telephoning abroad when one cannot dial direct 114
Time 161
Tourist information bulletin and, in winter, snow reports and avalanche bulletin 120
Weather report 162
Note: there is usually a surcharge on calls from hotels. To telephone to Switzerland, dial the initial code 010 followed by the country code 41, then the area code and subscriber number.

Time

Switzerland and the Principality of Liechtenstein observe Central European Time: *ie* they are one hour ahead of Greenwich Mean Time and six hours ahead of New York time. Swiss Summer

DIRECTORY

Time is one hour ahead of Central European Time: *ie* two hours ahead of GMT and seven hours ahead of New York Time.

Tipping

Generally speaking there is no need for tipping in hotels, restaurants, cafés, bars and hairdressing salons because a service charge is automatically added to the bill. However, a small additional tip is appropriate for exceptional service. Most taxi drivers include the service charge automatically, but it is wise to check. Otherwise, small tips are customary for porters and cloakroom attendants.

Toilets

Most Swiss toilets are clean and well looked after. They are indicated by a variety of signs, such as WC, *Toiletten* (in German), *Toilettes* (in French), or *Gabinetti* (in Italian). Women's lavatories are described as *Damen* or *Frauen, Femmes* or *Dames, Signore* or *Donne,* and men's as *Herren* or *Männer, Hommes* or *Messieurs, Signori* or *Uomini.*

Tourist Offices

Swiss National Tourist Offices
London Swiss National Tourist Office, Swiss Centre, 1 New Coventry Street, London W1V 8EE (tel: (0171) 734 1921)
New York Swiss National Tourist Office, Swiss Center, 608 Fifth Avenue, New York, NY 10020 (tel: (212) 757 5944)
San Francisco Swiss National Tourist Office, 250 Stockton Street, San Francisco, CA 94108, USA (tel: (415) 362 2260)
Sydney Swiss National Tourist Office, 203-233 New South Head

A spectacular way to enjoy a drink: above Lake Lugano

Road, Edgecliff, Sydney NSW 2027 (tel: (02) 326 1799)
Toronto Swiss National Tourist Office, Commerce Court, Toronto, Ontario, Canada M5L 1EB (tel: (416) 868 0584)

Useful Addresses in Switzerland

Schweizerische Verkehrszentrale (Swiss National Tourist Office - head office), Bellariastrasse 38, CH-8017 **Zürich** (tel: (01) 2881111).
Touring Club Suisse (TCS), 9 rue Pierre-Fatio, CH-1211 **Genève** 3 (tel: (022) 7371212).
Schweizer Alpenclub (Swiss Alpine club), Helvetiaplatz 4, CH-3005 **Bern** (tel: (031) 433611).
Schweizer Jugendherbergen Schaffhauserstr. 14 P.O. Box CH-8042 **Zürich** (tel: (01) 3601414).

Regional Tourist Offices

Grisons Verkehrsverein, Alexanderstrasse 24, CH-7001 **Chur** (tel: (081) 2542424).
Eastern Switzerland and the Principality of Liechtenstein Verkehrsverband, Bahnhofplatz 1a, CH-9001 **St Gallen** (tel: (071) 226262).
Central Switzerland Verkehrsverband, Alpenstrasse 1, CH-6002 **Luzern** (tel: (041) 511891).
Northwest Switzerland Verkehrsverein, Blumenrain 2, CH-4001 **Basel** (tel: (061) 255050).
Bernese Oberland Verkehrsverband, Jungfraustrasse 38, CH-3800 **Interlaken** (tel: (036) 222621).
Bernese Mittelland Verkehrsverband, Im Bahnhof CH-3001 **Bern** (tel: (031) 3111212).
Fribourg, Neuchâtel, Jura, Bernese Jura Union fribourgeoise du tourisme, 4 route de la Carrière, CH-1700 **Fribourg** 3 (tel: (037)245644); Fédération neuchâteloise du tourisme, Rue du Trésor 9, CH-2001 **Neuchâtel** (tel: (038) 251789) Office jurassien du tourisme, 12 place de la Gare, CH-2800 **Delémont** (tel: (066) 229777); Office du tourisme du Jura bernois, 26 avenue de la Liberté, CH-2740 **Moutier** (tel: (032) 936466).
Lac Léman Region Office du tourisme, 60 avenue d'Ouchy, CH-1006 **Lausanne** (tel: (021) 6177202).
Valais Union valaisanne du tourisme, rue Pré-Fleuri 6, CH-1950 **Sion** (tel: (027) 223161).
Ticino Ente Ticinese per il Turismo, via Lugano 12, CH-6501 **Bellinzona** (tel: (092) 257056).

LANGUAGE

Switzerland has four official languages: German (65 per cent), spoken in the central and eastern regions; French (18 per cent), in the west; Italian (10 per cent), in the south; and Romansch, a derivative of Latin and spoken by only 1 per cent, in the far southeast. English is widely spoken, but it is useful to know a few words and phrases in the local languages. On the next page are listed, in the three main languages, some words and expressions which should help the visitor to communicate with the Swiss in any part of the country, even if only on a basic level.

LANGUAGE

	German	**French**	**Italian**
good day	guten Tag	bonjour	buon giorno
please	bitte	s'il vous plait	per favore
thank you	danke	merci	grazie
yes/no	ja/nein	oui/non	si/no
excuse me	entschuldigen Sie	excusez-moi	mi scusi
do you speak English	sprechen Sie Englisch?	parlez-vous anglais?	parla inglese?
I don't understand	ich verstehe nicht	je ne comprends pas	non capisco
speak slowly	sprechen Sie langsam	parlez lentement	parli adagio
where is/are..?	wo ist/sind..?	où se… trouve(nt)..?	dov'è/dove sono..?
...the airport	der Flugplatz	l'aéroport	l'aeroporto
...the railway station	der Bahnhof	la gare	la stazione ferroviaria
a bank/ exchange	eine Bank/ Wechselstube	une banque/ change	una banca/ agenzia di cambio
...the police station	die Polizei	le poste de police	la polizia
...a pharmacy	eine Apotheke	une pharmacie	una farmacia
the toilet	die Toilette	les toilettes	i gabinetti
how much?	wieviel?	combien?	quant'è?
what is this?	was ist das?	qu'est-ce-que c'est?	cos'è questo?
when?	wann?	quand (à quelle heure)?	quando (a che ora)?
yesterday/ today/ tomorrow	gestern/ heute/ morgen	hier/ aujourd'hui/ demain	ieri/ oggi/ domani
Monday	Montag	lundi	lunedi
Tuesday	Dienstag	mardi	martedi
Wednesday	Mittwoch	mercredi	mercoledi
Thursday	Donnerstag	jeudi	giovedi
Friday	Freitag	vendredi	venerdi
Saturday	Samstag	samedi	sabato
Sunday	Sonntag	dimanche	domenica
open/closed	offen/ geschlossen	ouvert/fermé	aperto/chiuso
goodbye	auf Wiedersehen	au revoir	arrivederci

INDEX

INDEX/ACKNOWLEDGEMENTS

The Automobile Association would like to thank the following libraries for their assistance in the compilation of this book.

AA PHOTO LIBRARY 42/3 Kapellbrücke, Lucern (S. Day)

J ALLAN CASH PHOTOLIBRARY Page 19 Schaffhausen, 49 Arosa, 58 Valais, 70 Fribourg, 87 Vaduz, 108 Pool at Klosters.

INTERNATIONAL PHOTOBANK Front cover Grindelwald, page 6 Kleine Scheidegg, 11 Grindelwald, 20 Schaffhausen, 23 Zürich, 26 Bern, 31 Brienz, 33 Brunnen, 40 Jungfrau railway, 44/5 Wengen, 47 Wilderswil, 60 Locarno, 62 Lugano, 68 Matternorn, 77 Gruyères, 79 Lausanne, 80 Les Diablerets, 86 Villars, 100 Meal, 117 Jungfrau Glacier, 118 Village church, 122 Lake Lugano.

NATURE PHOTOGRAPHERS LTD
Page 90 Goldfinches (P R Sterry), 92/3 Yellow wood violet (P R Sterry), 94 Spring gentian (P R Sterry), 97 Alpine chough (P R Sterry), 98 Purple coltsfoot (P R Sterry), 99 Honey buzzard (M Muller).
SPECTRUM COLOUR LIBRARY Page 13 Basel, 15 Carnival, 36 Grindelwald, 39 Interlaken, 53 Klosters, 55 St Moritz, 66 Verbier, 84 Vevey, 103 Carnival, 107 Hikers, 121 Mountain railway, 124 Tessin

ZEFA PICTURELIBRARY 25 Bahnhofstrasse Zürich, 35 Wetterhorn, 51 Davos, 56 Ascona, 64 Saas-Fee, 65 Sion, 72 Genève, 82 Montreux, 105 Children, 112 Grindelwald, 115 Jungfrau glacier.

Contributors
For this revision:
Copy editor: Sheila Hawkins   Verifier: David Allsop
Thanks also to **Gerry Crawshaw** and the **TCS** (Touring Club Suisse) for their assistance.